THE PRINCE

THE PRINCE

JILLIAN DODD

Jillian Dodd Inc.
N. Redington Beach, FL

ISBN: 978-1-940652-96-2

THIS BOOK IS DEDICATED TO ALL THE
WRITERS WHO SPARKED MY
IMAGINATION AS A CHILD AND MADE
ME DREAM OF BEING A SPY SOMEDAY.

And to the people who

humored me.

Books by Jillian Dodd

The Keatyn Chronicles®
Stalk Me
Kiss Me
Date Me
Love Me
Adore Me
Hate Me
Get Me

Hollywood Love Series
Fame
Power
Money
Sex
Love

That Boy Series
That Boy
That Wedding
That Baby

The Love Series
Vegas Love
Broken Love

Spy Girl Series
The Prince
The Eagle
The Society

Falsehood of the tongue leads to that of the heart, and in time depraves all its good dispositions.
-Thomas Jefferson

PROLOGUE

A MAN IS being hung by his feet from the top of a sixteen-story building.

He tried to evade his pursuer but could not. The pursuer was like a ghost who would magically appear no matter where the man tried to hide.

And it is in moments like these that men experience clarity in their lives.

The dangling man knows he will die soon. And, still, he refuses to admit to the ghost that he had anything to do with the crime. After all, he was ordered to do so by a man no one dares to cross, for fear you will end up in a situation like the one he is now.

Fearing for his life.

He did not cross his employer, though. He simply made a mistake. Last night when he was three sheets to the wind, he may have been bragging about a job he did recently in Britain.

It was an easy job, kill a man who was hunting and make it look like a suicide. No one in the pub was surprised. The types that gathered at this establishment were all criminals of one form or another, but he'd gotten a big payday and it made him feel a few notches above the rest.

"Tell me who hired you," the ghost yells at him, threatening to let go.

The man shakes his head. If he tells, he will die—either by this man's hand or his employer's, and he'd much rather get dropped off this building than face what his employer would do to him. He should know. He's fulfilled numerous contracts with explicit instructions for a slow, painful death. Or worse, making them watch their families die first.

"If you tell me, I'll keep you safe," the ghost offers.

"*Nowhere* is safe from him!"

"Just give me his name. Atone for what you've done."

The man considers this. Would telling the ghost allow him to end up better in eternity?

He shakes his head again. "It's already been set in motion. No one can stop it now."

The man feels himself fall as the ghost lets go of one of his legs. Although he quickly discovers he only dropped slightly, it felt like many feet. He has a wife at home and an elderly mother. Even in death, his employer would punish him—by killing his family—if he thought he had been betrayed. But the ghost is good. He's clearly a highly trained spy, who may be the only one able to stop his employer.

"We can protect you! Tell me!"

He feels the man's grip slip, and in a flash of panic yells out, "Please, don't let go! I'll tell you! I'll tell you!"

The ghost pulls him to the safety of the roof then levels a gun at his chest. "Who hired you?"

"A man who is not in charge, but I overheard some things."

"Like what?"

"*It starts with Montrovia*," he tells the ghost. It's not all he knows, but hopefully it will be enough.

A relative peace overcomes him, and he now knows what he must do to protect his family.

It's the only way.

He leans backward and pitches himself over the ledge.

"Shit," the ghost mutters, putting his gun away and reaching for his phone.

"We were right. It's starting," he says to the man who answers.

"Do you have him in custody?"

"Sort of," he replies, looking down at the broken

body lying in the street.

"Is he alive?"

"Uh, not so much."

"Did you find out who hired him?" The voice sounds angry.

"As we suspected, it was a man who is not in charge. But he confessed to overhearing something."

"Dammit, you should have kept him alive. We need more information."

"He said enough. It starts with Montrovia."

The man on the other end goes silent. "I was hoping to give her more time."

"We can't wait any longer."

"I'll make the call," he says reluctantly.

MISSION: DAY ONE

MY MOTHER IS on her knees in our living room.

She's pleading at me with her eyes. Although the man standing in front of her thinks she's begging not to be shot with the suppressed handgun he's pointing at her, I know she's really begging for me not to do what I'm about to do—shoot the man myself.

She closes her eyes as I pull the trigger.

But I'm too late.

A tiny hole forms in the center of her forehead as blood sprays onto the couch behind her.

I watch in stunned horror, a scream rising in my throat even though I know I should keep quiet.

The man turns to face me. He's clutching his shoulder, which I must have hit.

His eyes bore into mine. Eyes I will never forget.

Then he turns his gun on me.

"X, wake up," my study hall professor says, pushing on my shoulder. Even on Sundays, we have mandatory study periods.

"I'm sorry. I was up late studying," I say smoothly.

"The Dean would like you to report to his office immediately."

I stand up and smooth out my uniform—which, not surprisingly, is all black—grab my backpack, and head down the hall, my dream still at the forefront of my mind.

X has been my name since I came to Blackwood six years ago after my parents were killed. I slide my hand down the thick chair rail and take in the polished beauty that is Blackwood Academy, the stately mansion that has been my home since then. Although to the outside world it appears to be an elite boarding school for only the wealthiest of students, it's not really. If Hogwarts was for young wizards who show talent with magic, Blackwood is for students who show exceptional skills in disciplines like martial arts, languages, computer hacking, and rule-breaking. Talents that our government can harness and train.

As I descend the grand iron staircase, I start to worry.

Last night, I may not have actually been studying. I may have been hooking up with S, who told me his real name is Josh Bentley after we slept together. He wasn't my first. At Blackwood, dating isn't allowed, but we aren't expected to deny our sexual desires. As long as we are not in violation of other rules like curfew, sex is fine, even considered a great way to release tension—which means the standard pickup line here is, *Wanna blow off some steam?* And that works for me.

I know I'm going to have to end things with Josh because last night when he held me in his arms, he dared to whisper those three little words—sweet words most girls long to hear but are the death of a relationship at Blackwood. Here, we're taught to thrive on our own. To not crave emotional entanglements.

Last night, I failed in that respect. I liked hearing it.

But I'm chalking up my emotion to the events that preceded his words. All the students had been woken up yesterday at 0500 for a mission enactment. Twelve hours later—muddy, hungry, and exhausted—I used a sniper rifle to kill the target and retrieve the stolen data. Josh and I had worked together all day using our tracking abilities while being hunted. Just staying alive—as in not getting hit with a rubber bullet—is a feat. Completing the mission is a rare thing. Our enemies were two former graduates who had never been beat.

After we'd scarfed down food in the mess hall, Josh and I celebrated by sneaking out with a 1974 bottle of Bordeaux I nicked from the school's wine cellar.

And I have a feeling someone is missing that bottle.

I'm only a few weeks from graduation, and although it's not that unusual for me to be sent to the Dean's office for various misdemeanors, I've been particularly careful lately because after graduation I want to be a field operative for a covert agency. Because it's my best chance of finding the man from my dream—and killing him.

When I get to the bottom of the stairs, I turn right then lift the brass knocker which contains a retinal scanner. My eye gets scanned and then the door responds with a click, letting me know I can open it.

"Hello, Xanthamum," the Dean's perpetually cheerful assistant says to me. She dresses like a grandmother and makes up a new name every time she sees you, but we all know it's just a ruse. The woman retired from the CIA over ten years ago and is still a crack shot. "Go on in. He's waiting for you."

I give her a smile, hoping she will say more. She likes to gossip about the goings on at school. But in this case, she gives me a wave toward the door.

"Hello, sir," I say to the Dean, by way of announcing my arrival.

He looks up from his book. "Have a seat."

I sit down in a well-worn leather chair across from his desk. If I'm being honest, I love the Dean's office. It's a former library and is loaded with shelf after shelf of books. And the Dean has been a sort of father figure to me, like if your dad was the type of guy to push you to do better at holding your breath under water, hitting a target the size of a peanut from one hundred feet, hacking into the Pentagon, and kicking the shit out of your jujitsu instructor.

"It's my understanding that you are a good dancer," he says.

Shit, he definitely knows I was dancing with Josh in his room after curfew. And by dancing, I mean having sex. But spies are trained not to follow the rules. To complete the mission whatever it takes. We are trained liars. So I reply coolly, "Of course, all of Blackwood's students take finishing class."

"I'm referring to the fact that you can actually dance well, like at a club."

Crap. He knows my friend M and I sneak out to hear DJ Magic whenever he's in town, which would be a worse offense than the wine.

I'm so dead.

"Uh, sure. I can dance."

"You've been called out."

Called out? Who ratted me out? Probably M's roommate. She hates that M and I sneak out. It's not our fault we don't require much sleep and like to have some fun occasionally.

"And you're popular with the young men of Blackwood," he continues.

So I've maybe a few short-term relationships with a

couple of them.

"Uh . . ."

"What I'm saying is that you're pretty, you look good in a bikini, and know how to dance—so you're being called out."

"I'm in trouble for that?"

"No. You are being called to duty for those reasons."

I sit up straighter. Wait?! He has an assignment for me? "But what about graduation?" I ask. Graduation consists of a senior skip day where we track real criminals, and I've been really looking forward to it.

"This is more important." He hands me a black envelope. The back has a red monogrammed seal with a letter X on it.

"Is this from where I think it's from?"

"Yes, they've been watching your progress."

Oh. My. Gosh. My first assignment. I wonder what I'm going to be tasked to do. Sneak in the Kremlin, assassinate a terrorist, find a nuclear device, save the world?

He nods expectantly at me. I stop wondering about my mission and look at the envelope again.

I know the drill. Open my orders, commit them to memory, destroy them.

Your **mission, should you choose to** *accept it:*
Protect **the heir to the throne of Montrovia,** *uncover* **the person or persons behind the plot**

to assassinate him in order to take control of this geographically important sovereign nation, and *eliminate* the threat.

Get close to the hottest Prince on the planet *and* work for Black X, the double-black covert group so secret even the President of the United States is on a need-to-know basis?

I accept.

I think about what he said about me looking good in a bikini. Do they want me to hookup with this Prince in order to protect him? Are you kidding me? I'm valedictorian. I have the school's highest scores in everything from parkour to the number of ways I can kill a man.

I frown as I'm burning my orders in the fireplace. "Sir, may I speak freely about my assignment?"

"I'm afraid I'm not privy to your orders. My job was to help choose the student best fitted for the task based on the parameters given to me."

"And one of those parameters was that I look good in a bathing suit?"

He chuckles. "In this situation, my dear, they need an operative who is not only the best and brightest but one who can also demand male attention. Your handler is waiting for you outside. You leave immediately."

"But I need to go pack. Tell people goodbye."

"I'm afraid there's no time." He stands up and, in an uncustomary show of emotion, hugs me briefly.

"Godspeed, X."

AFTER SHE LEAVES his office, the Dean opens a drawer, takes out a bottle of bourbon, and sets it on his desk.

He's never questioned his orders but, in this case, he can't help it. He's been dreading this day for the last six years when he was called out of retirement to become the Dean of Blackwood Academy.

His hands shake as he pours the amber-colored liquid into a glass.

Blackwood Academy sounded good on paper. They sold it to him well. He'd get to train young spies. Continue to serve his country.

The Russians have had programs like this for years, taking orphans, delinquents, or high IQ students and training them. Stripping them of their names and families. Teaching them to be killing machines. To have no consciences. To only do what they are told is best for their country.

Blackwood would be different—a combination of higher education, clandestine training, boot camp, and finishing school. Its graduates would be elite, intelligent, and most of all, lethal.

What he never expected was for them to send her.

At only twelve.

Her beautiful mother had been shot, execution style, in front of her by the most deadly assassin in the world, a man known only as The Priest. And somehow, she managed to shoot and wound the assassin, fight him off, and then escape. A feat not even the most seasoned agent had ever accomplished.

Two days later, she defied death again, when a bomb blew up her father's car.

She wasn't allowed to attend their funerals. Spies don't have funerals. They get a star on a wall in an office deep underground and a few moments of silence.

This he knows. He's attended too many of those moments over the years.

He brings the glass to his lips and takes a small sip, enjoying the way the liquid burns, reminding him he's still alive.

Even though most of the world believes him to be dead.

During her time at Blackwood, he's grown to care deeply for X and feels more proud of her than he knew possible. He was hard on her, but she has amazed him with her abilities at every turn.

He wanted to tell her the truth today. The truth about her. The truth about him. The truth about her parents.

The phone on his desk rings, startling him.

He hears a series of clicks, knowing he's being put through to a secure connection.

"Well?" the voice asks.

He takes another drink, greedily gulping it so he can bring himself to say the words he's been dreading since that day. "Spy Girl is a go."

"Do you think she's ready?"

"With her genes and my training, what do you think?"

"You sound defiant, old man. I take it this mission is difficult for you."

"She's ready. I've done everything I can. She's the best I've ever trained."

"And the only one who mattered. Do you think she will be able to attract the Prince's attention and protect him?"

"That's her mission. Of course, she will. Although, I think she was a little disappointed."

"Why?"

"She would have preferred something more exciting. She wants to save the world."

"And avenge her mother's death. If those behind the plot to overthrow the monarchy are serious, The Priest is who they would hire."

"The Priest? How would they hire him? He's dead. Rumor has it he was double crossed by whoever hired him to kill her mother."

"I'd say that's debatable. If he were still alive, do you think he'd recognize her?"

"If he were alive, I'd be more worried about her recognizing him."

"Why's that?"

"I'm not sure how she would react. And I thought we were going to send her on a few test missions to start."

"Things have progressed, and we can't wait any longer. If she fails, we'll deal with the repercussions. You and I both know this is a whole lot bigger than one small country."

When the line goes dead, he drains the rest of the glass.

And wonders what he's done.

I WALK OUT of the Dean's office feeling elated. I'm going to meet my handler. My first ever, real handler. The person who will do whatever I need in the field.

I survey the area looking for him, but only see a guy about my age, who is way too good looking to be a handler. Usually handlers are decrepit retired spies.

But then I see a distinguished looking older gentleman who reaches his white-gloved hand out to me.

"Pleased to meet you. I'm Ellis." He hands me an envelope. "Here are your credentials, driver's license, passport, credit cards, and bio. Let's get going. We don't have much time."

Ellis opens the back door of a Bentley. The guy hops in before me. Obviously, finishing school was not part of his training.

"Um, who are you?" I ask. I'm sort of hoping he's supposed to be my boyfriend. That would be an assignment I could put all my energy into.

"Read your bio," he tells me, putting headphones on and virtually ignoring me.

Rude asshole.

As we're sitting silently in the back of the chauffeured car, I think of the neatly typed words. The words I've been waiting years to read.

This is it. My first assignment. The first step in my plan. I'll get a few successful missions under my belt then I'll use my abilities to hunt down the man who murdered my mother and kill him.

I smile to myself at the thought, then pull out the papers and start reading about Montrovia.

Geographically important is right. Trillions of dollars of goods are moved through the Strait of Montrovia. Specifically trillions of dollars of oil they allow every country to move across its waters.

So basically, I'm supposed to seduce the Prince and somehow keep him from getting killed. Honestly, I'd rather chase a terrorist. He's a freaking Prince. He will be impossible to get near.

I flip the page and see a photo of my target as well as his statistics. HRH Lorenzo Giovanni Baptiste Vallenta. Twenty-three, six-feet tall, dark haired, and very easy on the eyes. Numerous articles pertain to his exploits; with sailing, polo ponies, fast cars, and fast women among his favored hobbies. Apparently, it's not yet been publicly announced, but the Prince's father is ill and not expected to recover. So the fact that someone has already developed a plan to assassinate him to take control of the country means whoever is behind the plot is well connected. I study the order of succession. The King. The Prince. Then his cousin, The Duchess of Cordova, and her sister, The Countess of Cordova.

I take out my new credentials and study them.

I am Huntley Penelope "Penny" Bond-Von Allister.

"Are you kidding me?" I say out loud. "Did they really name me after Ethan Hunt from *Mission Impossible* and James Bond from *007*?"

Ellis snickers in the front seat.

I elbow the guy sitting next to me. He glares at me then takes off his headphones. "What?"

"Do I look like a *Penny*?"

"Not really, but that's what I'll be calling you. It's in my notes."

"You will *not* be calling me that. I'll go by Huntley. What is your name?"

"Keep reading." He leaves his headset off this time and stares out the window, continuing to ignore me.

"Who makes this shit up?" I mutter.

Actually, I know the answer to that question. The team does. Behind every good spy is an equally strong support team. Researchers, weapons specialists, logistics, finance, etc. They call them *Housekeeping*. They have prepared my backstory, my travel documents, packed my bags for the trip, will have a residence acquired at our destination, and have vetted my credentials.

I keep reading.

I'm taking a break from school to see the world with my brother, Aristotle "Ari" Bradford-Von Allister. We are going to Montrovia to spend time together after our billionaire father, the reclusive Ares Von Allister, passed away.

I study the guy sitting next to me. He's about six feet tall, solidly built but still lean. If I had to guess, he's got nice muscles under the heavy flannel shirt he's wearing. His hair is about the same color as mine, a dirty blonde—heavy on the dirty. His eyes are a similar hazel with a strong Roman nose and long face. His hair is cut short on the sides and long on the top in the trend newly favored by hipsters across the world. Whoever cast us as brother and sister did a good job. We actually look a lot alike.

"Are you Ari?"

"Yes."

"You're going to have to loosen up if you want anyone to believe you're a billionaire playboy."

"Finish reading," he says, his eyes looking equal parts lethal and sexy.

"Well, this is interesting. We just met at the reading of our father's will. The father neither of us had ever met. In order to inherit his billions, we have to spend the next six months getting to know each other."

He nods. "It's a good cover. And Ares did just pass. So the timing is perfect."

I take a moment to study my new brother. His stiff posture suggests some kind of military training, but he also has the air of someone raised with a silver spoon in his mouth. This contradiction intrigues me, and I want to know where and how he trained. Our legend says that I'm twenty and he's twenty-one. Since that's not my real age, I'm assuming it's not his either.

We've leased a villa overlooking the Mediterranean in the glitzy Montrovian city, Cap de Playa Antilles. Better known as Cap. It's a playground for the ultra-rich, boasting a harbor large enough to handle the priciest of yachts, an elegant casino complex, luxurious hotels, world-class restaurants, exclusive designer shops, an ornate opera house, and streets littered with exotic cars. The town is a magnet for glitzy and glittering events, home to an elite polo team, tennis championships, and a Formula One race, which happens to be taking place next weekend.

Our chauffeur and butler, Ellis, will be traveling with us. He's about sixty, and when I look at him in the rear view mirror, he gives me a discreet wink.

Then he speaks. "Are you through reading your dossier? Have you committed the details to memory?"

The details he's referring to are things like my name, birthdate, and social security number. Of more importance, the phone number that will connect me directly to Black X and a series of authentication code words. Child's play.

"Yes," I say, confidently.

"Good, because we have some shopping to do."

Ari groans, so I smack him.

But instead of shopping at a store, it seems the store has come to us. Upon arrival at our three-bedroom suite in a posh D.C. hotel, we are greeted by racks of clothing and two women both named Kate.

Kate Number One says, "You can call me Dr. Kate."

"What are you a doctor of?" I ask politely.

"I have my undergrad in luxury marketing from NYU and a doctorate in Anthropology. It's my job to make sure you look the part. I'm on your Housekeeping team along with my colleague, Kate."

Kate Number Two says, "If you call the private concierge number that is in your phone, you'll be speaking directly with me. I'll arrange anything you need on site. As you were told, we've leased a beautiful villa that comes with a full staff. We've shipped over all sorts of goodies for you. Once you step foot in Montrovia, you will be Penny and Ari."

"Um, *Huntley*."

She studies me. "You're right. I can't picture you as a Penny. Anyway, other than Ellis, you are on your own. Any information you come across will be relayed to us through secure messaging, and if the shit hits the fan, you each have emergency protocol."

"Let's get you into the wardrobes we've selected to make sure everything fits. We have a tailor on standby, and then you both have appointments at the spa downstairs. Hairstylists and makeup will be brought in to prep you for the event tonight."

"There was no mention of an event in my packet," Ari states.

"Rule follower," I say under my breath.

Dr. Kate says, "You're going to the Smithsonian Gala. We've got you seated with Peter Prescott and his model of the week. Peter is—"

"The son of Malcolm Prescott," Ari says. "Prescott Industries' self-made billionaire. His conglomerates rebuild after a war, and he's a big contributor to President Hillford's campaign."

Kate does a little clap. "Correct, Ari, you've been studying."

I wonder why I haven't been allowed to study.

"Also at the table will be Peter's Yale buddy, Daniel Spear."

"Son of Vice President Spear," I add. At least I know

something. Although it's really not that spectacular. Every woman in America—and most other countries—would recognize the gold-medal winning Olympic swimmer with his blinding white teeth, piercing blue eyes, crooked grin, and a body made of steel—based on his latest men's fitness magazine cover, which may have been tossed around my dorm room and drooled over. Dr. Kate smiles at me, so I continue. "They are our entry into Montrovian society, I take it?"

"Yes, your mission for tonight is to make friends with Peter and invite him to join you for a weekend of partying. Daniel is an acquaintance of the Prince. Although, he isn't likely to go to Montrovia, knowing him can't hurt. It all depends on the two of you. Are you charming and believable enough to pull this off?"

Ari glances in my direction, sizing me up.

"Have you scheduled some time for Huntley and I to get to know each other before the event?" Ari asks the Kates.

"We're on a tight schedule, but you'll be alone from five until you leave for the event at promptly seven p.m. You can use that time as you see fit." Kate smirks, and I know she's thinking of exactly how she'd choose to use that time if she were me.

I stifle a smile. Good. Ari's hotness is good for our mission.

But he's totally not my type. I can already tell he's

way too uptight.

The Vice President's son, on the other hand, has dated everyone from pop stars to the local stripper. He's much more my type. Fast, carefree, and easy. Ari looks like he requires care and feeding. High maintenance with a capital H. The kind of guy who would annoy the crap out of me.

Which I'm told brothers usually do.

ARI AND I don't have time to chat as planned. Between spa appointments and tailoring, we're barely ready in time. Fortunately, while I was getting my toes, nails, and hair done, I was able to read more about Montrovia on my phone. I studied the country's history, maps of the capital, blueprints of the castle, and the folklore. I've memorized the shops, read up on the Formula One drivers, and even found a cool article on all the secret passageways in the castle as well as learned the ghost of a former king is said to haunt the stables.

We arrive at the event by chauffeured limousine. The museum is bathed in a soft pink light. A red carpet creeps up the stairs. Hollywood stars, music industry moguls, models, billionaires, politicians, socialites, professional athletes, and artists all come together to support one of the country's greatest institutions. A place I could spend days in with all its history. But most of the people are here to be seen. It's a splashy and glitzy event that marks the end of the society season.

The fact that on my first covert mission I will be photographed seems odd to me. Spies are taught to remain nameless and faceless. One of our most important classes at Blackwood was how to avoid being photographed on all the surveillance cameras around the world—your head down, a scarf, a hood, the tilt of your head.

"Maybe we should avoid the red carpet hoopla and sneak in through the kitchen, Ari."

He holds out his elbow. "We're going in the front and establishing our cover."

"Aren't you worried about how this will affect future missions?"

"I think this is our future mission. If we succeed, there will be many more missions together. It's brilliant, really. Being undercover in plain sight. So smile for the cameras."

I wrap my hand around his elbow and allow him to escort me up the stairs. We smile and pose for the cameras when told to, and as we enter the reception, there are already numerous people. A waiter presents us with a tray of champagne, and we each take a glass.

"To us," Ari says, raising his flute. "And to our great country."

WE ARE ALLOWED to roam the museum and mingle

before the event. Somehow, people already know who Ari and I are and offer us condolences on our father's passing.

Mostly, these seem to be the politicians.

"Ari, don't you find it a little odd that people know us and know who our father was when you and I met less than nine hours ago?"

"When were you told about our mission?" he asks me.

"Nine hours ago, when were you?"

"Three weeks ago. A few days after he passed."

"What do you know about him?"

"Not much, but I know his company worked with the government on numerous projects. He was a brilliant inventor, but a recluse for the past few years. We inherited his D.C. estate. You should see the place. It has a research facility that was second to none."

"Ari, we didn't really inherit it. It's just our cover."

He shakes his head. "No, it's our new life."

I PONDER THAT as we're being herded into the rotunda where we will dine. We've yet to meet our dining partners for the evening, but I have been given numerous business cards so I can invest some of my new money and was told I should consider a career in politics. I met a famous actor and had my ass grabbed by a lecherous old senator, whose wife informed me that he meant no harm.

The man's lucky he still has an arm.

When Ari and I arrive at our table, Peter Prescott and his date, a model named Allie Peterson, are already seated. Ari and I introduce ourselves as the Von Allisters.

"Sorry to hear about your father," Peter says. "He and my dad worked together back in the day."

Really? Why the hell wasn't this in my packet? But I just found out he was my father. I shouldn't know anything about him. Other than his net worth.

"I'd love to hear about that. We never knew him."

"You never knew your father?" the model asks.

"Haven't you seen the papers?" Peter asks, squinting his eyes at her like she's an idiot. I'd wipe that smug look off his face if I were dating him. Of course, I probably wouldn't date an arrogant asshole.

She kisses him on the cheek. "You know I don't read them. All bad news. It's depressing."

I decide to fill her in. "Ari and I just met at the reading of our father's will. We didn't know he was our father until we were notified by his attorney."

"You're looking at our country's two newest billionaires," Peter proclaims.

Her eyes brighten. "Oh. Well, congratulations."

I wince. So do Ari and Peter. But secretly I love this clueless, beautiful girl.

Peter whispers something to her. She frowns then

looks at Ari and gives him a dazzling smile. "I'm sorry. That didn't come out right. I'm sorry for your loss."

We are joined by Senator Bill Callan and his wife, Sissy. He chairs the Senate Appropriations Committee and is known as a good friend of the director of the CIA, Mike Burnes. He shakes my hand, also offers his condolences, and introduces us to the actor Rob Howden and his wife, Angie. Bill's secretary apparently doesn't warrant an introduction. She sits silently at the table on her phone with the air of someone doing something very important, but she blushes when I catch her scrolling through her Instagram feed.

We are all seated at the table making small talk about the new exhibit we toured.

The chair to my left is still empty when I get my first glimpse of Daniel.

He's rushing toward us, buttoning his jacket; his cheeks flush. I half expect him to be zipping his pants. He looks like he's been involved in a coat room quickie. His hair is mussed. His blue eyes sparkling.

"Sorry, I'm late," he says to the table. "My parents decided last minute to attend the event and made me ride with them. Traveling with the Secret Service is a bitch."

He shakes his buddy Peter's hand and gives him a slap on the back, air kisses Allie, and then works his way around the table shaking everyone's hands.

When he gets to me, he says, "I'm Daniel Spear."

"I'm Huntley Von Allister, and this is my brother Ari."

A speaker on the stage addresses the group, so we all quickly take our seats.

Daniel's piercing blue eyes continue to hold mine, occasionally flitting across the curves of my red gown. His eyes are mesmerizing, a warm lush shade of lapis with lighter flecks of cerulean. His eyes speak of oceans and tropics, and it's not surprising he's talented in the water. I imagine that Neptune, the Roman God of the Sea, would have had eyes just like his.

We toast to the event and let the senator and his wife carry most of the table's dinner conversation.

After dessert, the talk turns to travel spots of the rich and famous. Sissy and the senator are vacationing at their six thousand square foot "cottage" in the balmy Cayman Islands starting next week, and Allie is headed to Puerto Rico tomorrow for a popular sports magazine's bikini shoot.

The senator and his wife excuse themselves, along with the actor and his spouse.

"We're going to Montrovia," Ari says.

"Montrovia?" Daniels replies. "I just happen to be pals with the Prince of Montrovia. Haven't seen him in a couple years. I'll tell you what, though. He knows how to party. I never thought I'd recover from our night out."

"A prince, huh?" I tease.

"Don't start dreaming of a royal wedding just yet," Daniel teases back. "You'd have a lot of competition. Me, I'm easy."

"So I've read in the tabloids."

"Who is accompanying you on this trip?" Allie asks.

"It's just me and Ari. We're going to have some brother-sister bonding time."

Daniel's blue eyes smolder as he whispers to me, "Maybe it's time to go visit my old friend. Although, if I go, you know we're going to sleep together."

"I do love a good slumber party. Maybe I can braid your hair," I tease, tousling his dark, shaggy locks.

"When do we leave?" he asks.

"Tomorrow."

"Mode of transportation?"

"Well, if you're coming with, why don't we make a splash in Air Force Two?"

"You know I could make that happen."

"You talk a big game."

"And I deliver the goods." He smirks and raises an eyebrow at me. Gosh, this guy is a flirt. I love it.

"My prediction is that the Prince, who you claim to be friends with, won't remember you."

An amused smile plays on his lips. "I'm hard to forget."

"So you go both ways, huh?"

"What? No!"

I grin. "I'm just screwing with you."

"Not yet, Huntley, but soon you will be."

He grabs my phone, enters his number as *AirForce2* and says, "I'll be in touch." Then he excuses himself from the table.

Ari and Peter are talking exotic cars.

"That's why we're going, really. To hit the car show and the Formula One race. One of the things on Ari's bucket list."

"I'd love to go to Montrovia," Allie gushes. "We should go too, Peter."

"It's race weekend. No way we'd find a hotel room."

"You're welcome to stay at our villa," I suggest.

"That would be amazing!" she says, then turns to Peter. "Peter, you could come to my photo shoot, and we could leave from there." She gives him a little pout. "Please, baby."

Peter's face softens, and he gives her a sweet smile. "I hate to say no to you, but I have other plans."

Allie huffs at him then switches to Daniel's vacated spot next to me and gives me a girly rundown of Montrovia. She seems to know all about the place even though she's never been there. She goes on about what kind of clothes I should take, all the amazing yachts there, and how her publicist could get us into some A-List parties. I suppose when you have a body like hers, getting invites is probably easy.

"Have you and Peter dated long?"

"About three weeks. I'm not sure he's all that serious about me, though," she admits. "He likes models."

"I've heard he's a bit of a playboy."

"Yes, me too. He's so sweet though, and the lifestyle of a billionaire's son is crazy. I grew up on a farm in Illinois."

"I know what you mean. I just inherited that kind of money. I'm still in shock."

"Well, better to have it than to date it, if you know what I mean. Your brother is pretty cute."

"Uh, thank you."

"You two look alike. I see the family resemblance. Let's go to the bar and get a drink. Meet some more people."

I'm not sure, but by *people*, I think she's possibly shopping for men. Peter may be using her for her beauty, but she's using him as well. I guess I shouldn't judge. My job is to use people to get what I want. She seems really nice, though. If I wasn't who I am, I think we could be friends. Ari's words earlier about this being our life play back in my head. I wonder if he's right. Could there be more to this mission than I have been told?

Allie grabs my elbow and leads me to the restroom, where we touch up our lipstick and then head to the bar.

"That Daniel is quite a looker. He seemed very interested in you. Like, he didn't even look at me. Which is something I'm not used to."

"Do you believe his story about showing up with his parents? Looked to me like he just rolled out of bed."

"I hope he wasn't alone. That would be a shame. Don't you think he's cute?"

"He's like sex on a stick."

"I do like a big stick," she giggles, downing a glass of champagne.

"Care to dance?" a velvety voice says into my ear.

I don't have to turn around to know it's him.

"Do you mind?" I ask Allie.

"Oh, no," she says, latching on to Ari who is with Daniel. "Your brother can keep me company."

"I'd love to," I say to Daniel, taking his hand.

WE DANCE CLOSE, his hard body pressed against mine, and his lips nuzzling my neck. I suppose in some ways being a covert operative and going undercover is much like an actress playing a role. And although I know my role is to become friendly with Daniel, friendly takes on a whole new meaning when he lowers his lips to my neck and nips at it.

He turns me on. Plain and simple. While my mind is calculating different scenarios in which Daniel can further help my mission, my body is highly recommending that I sleep with him.

It's like I'm one of those cars, that all you have to do is push to start. And Daniel revs my motor further when he whispers in my ear, "I'm hungry. Would you want to go back to my place and have a real dinner?"

I know I'd like to feast on him.

I nod yes, tell Ari not to wait up, and before I know it, I'm in a limo staring at Daniel's hella good hair, his perfect profile, and his jawline of delicious scruff.

I was taught to exploit an opponent's weaknesses, and it's quite clear I'm going to need a much closer inspection to find anything weak on Daniel. From his strong, chiseled jaw down to a thick neck and broad shoulders. All of him is hard and muscular.

Which is probably what makes his brilliant blue eyes look so sweet and his lips look so soft and lush.

DANIEL'S TOWN HOUSE is incredible, an old brownstone on a prestigious street lined with embassies.

"Is this your parents' house?"

"No, it was my grandparents'. I inherited it last year. Isn't it great?"

I nod. The home is old with thick crown moldings, wood floors, finials, wood and stone fireplaces, lots of wainscoting and marble. But all the furnishings are a healthy mix of modern and antiques.

"I like what you've done to the place. You've kept all the original details but brought in modern furniture."

I'm rewarded with a smile and a peek of a dimple on his right side.

"I think it's my new goal in life to see your other dimple," I tell him.

He has a cocky smirk and a body built for all kinds of naughtiness, but his eyes are warm and tender.

At Blackwood, my professors couldn't find my weakness, but I might be looking at it right now—a pair of intense blue eyes.

"I only have one dimple." He holds a plethora of takeout menus in front of my face. "Pick one."

"And here I thought that was just a ploy to get me back to your place. I'm a little disappointed. Allie was regaling me with what she's read in the tabloids about you. All your tricks, *Air Force Two*."

He sets the menus down and studies my face, his blue eyes boring into mine. "I don't need tricks to get a girl to sleep with me."

And I don't doubt it.

He lowers his eyes to the menus and pulls a few out. "Let's get rid of the healthy options. I'm in the mood to be bad."

Oh gosh, me too, Daniel, me too. I'm going to drag him back to the bedroom even if it means I'll have to overcome and restrain him to do it. Those thoughts alone set my panties ablaze. And he's yet to kiss me.

He finally settles on a pizza menu.

"Best thick crust in the city. Anything you don't like on a pizza?"

"No anchovies. No onions. Other than that, I'm game for *anything*."

My answer is rewarded with the single dimple punctuating a small smile. A line like that at Blackwood would have earned me a lot more than a smile. It would have either gotten me four hours of wilderness survival training or thrown on a guy's dorm bed and wonderfully attacked.

I have a moment of self-doubt.

Maybe he really just wanted a dinner companion?

"So, Montrovia, huh?"

"Yeah. It's first up on the list."

"There's a list?"

"Yes, of all the places and things we'd like to see and do." I don't mention that *he* has rocketed straight to the top of the all the things I want to do.

Preferably now.

Like, right now.

I consider stripping off my clothes just to see what would happen, but when his stomach growls I realize he really is hungry. And if—no, when—I end up in bed with him, the last thing I want is for him not to have enough fuel for that amazing body. With all those muscles, he must burn like a thousand calories a minute just staring into space. I remember reading an article that said he eats like ten thousand calories a day when he's training.

"They said it will be about thirty minutes," he tells me after placing our order. "Want to play some Xbox?"

The night is going downhill quickly. He wants to play video games with me?

I tap my perfectly manicured nails on the island in response. I look down at my evening gown, the red color a contrast to my blonde hair, the straps highlighting my cleavage and the fabric floating over my curves.

If Daniel wants to be my friend, so be it. I'm going to be the sexiest best friend he's ever had.

I remind myself I'm on a mission but, in my mind, sleeping with Daniel has just become an integral part of that mission.

And I must not fail.

He plops down on the couch and pats the seat next to him as he readies the gaming controls.

I stop by his fridge, grab a couple beers, and hand him one when I sit down in the exact spot he patted, allowing the silk covering my thigh to brush against him. He hands me a controller and points to a list of games on the screen.

"Choose one."

I scroll through the list while he's busy staring at my cleavage.

Fortunately, I find what I'm looking for. It's a very

popular game that allows you to go on missions either by yourself, with a partner, or as a team. Only a few people know that this game started out as a teaching and training program for students at Blackwood Academy.

And I'm the best.

When I click on it, Daniel's eyes light up.

"This is a really complex game," he says, probably expecting me to choose something like Mario Kart.

I shrug noncommittally. I'm pretty sure this game is some kind of a litmus test. Daniel's way of screening girls. Which is odd. Never once in all the accounts I've read of his hookups have I read about there being pizza and Battleground involved.

We opt to go into battle together rather than against each other. And although the competitor in me wanted to go head-to-head and kill him in the game, my lady parts remind me that might be bad for his ego, which may have an adverse effect on his performance in bed.

I'm kicking butt in the game and, although we are partners against the bad guys, I'm amassing points at about a three-to-one ratio to his.

He pauses the game and slides out of his jacket. "I can't move in this monkey suit," he says. "Undo my tie, will you?"

I oblige, as I'm sure any girl would when asked to remove an article of his clothing—although, I was hoping for his pants.

He undoes his top two buttons and rolls up his shirt-sleeves, getting comfortable. And serious.

Which makes me smile.

His forearms flex as he takes the controller and continues the game. This round our score is more even, mostly because I'm obsessing over his muscles and not giving the game my all.

He's cursing, banging on the controller, and pulling up his weapons cache trying desperately to even the score.

My dress becomes increasingly uncomfortable and, in theory, could be hindering *my* performance.

I pause the game.

"What are you doing?"

"Give me your shirt," I instruct.

He just squints his eyes at me, so I lean over, unbutton it, and strip it off him.

And I'm trying hard not to drool.

Fine. A photo much like this one, where he's lounging on a couch shirtless may, in fact, be hanging in M's dorm room.

I stand and turn my back to him. The back of my dress is cut low and held in place by a short zipper that dives from my waist down to my ass.

"Unzip me, please."

He curses under his breath but complies.

I slide out of the dress, my back still to him. I'm

wearing a minute red satin G-string and nothing else. I was going to put my hand across my chest but decide not to. I mean, we're friends, and they're just boobs. No big deal.

Besides, I can do a few litmus tests of my own. If it weren't for the testosterone that oozes off him in waves, I'd think maybe he was gay.

I give him an eyeful of boobage as I lift his shirt off the couch and put it on. It covers my undies nicely and looks hot with my heels. I plop back down, even going so far as to unfurl my legs across his coffee table and cross them in a way that shows off my sky-high black pumps, whose red soles match my dress and lipstick.

Daniel is studying me closely. A quick glance at the bulge in his pants reaffirms my intel on his testosterone levels. I'm contemplating commanding him to remove them, so I can put them on, too, when the doorbell rings announcing our pizza delivery.

Make that *pizzas*. He ordered two.

Upon seeing my quizzical expression, he shrugs and throws one in the fridge. "One for now. One for breakfast."

"Shouldn't you be eating egg whites with spinach or something?"

He chuckles and sets the box in front of us then holds a gooey piece up to my mouth. I take a bite, savoring the combination of cheese, spicy sausage, roasted red peppers, and sweet pineapple.

"Mmm. This is my new favorite pizza," I groan.

He hands me the piece and takes his own, ripping into it.

His ferocity is hot.

I savor another bite then pull my legs up onto the couch crisscross style, being careful not to stab myself with my heels. I mentally kick myself realizing this is probably not nearly as sexy a position as having my long, tan legs sprawled across his table, but when he glances down and the dimple forms, I stay put.

I demolish piece number one and reach for the box. I might be amassing points faster, but he's winning the eating game, having mowed through three pieces already.

His appetite for food seemingly quelled, he holds a piece to my mouth again. His cerulean eyes remind me of the deep blue of a starry night sky. He is staring at my lips, wrapped around the crust.

"I'm glad you like the pizza," he states, his gaze moving downward. "You're good at Battleground. You should know I don't like to lose. We may not be leaving this couch tonight."

"Fine with me," I say, my desire growing as I care less about this stupid game.

I unzip his pants and proceed to straddle him.

Our lips collide, and he annihilates my mouth with his tongue. He's treating my mouth much like he did the video game—full on siege.

As he kisses his way down my neck, I move my hips against him.

He pats the couch for his pants, finds his wallet, and takes out a condom.

Things happen quickly and I can feel him smile into my neck when it's over and I practically collapse into a heap on top of him.

My tiredness is quickly abated when he picks me up, flips me over, and wraps my legs around his waist. I shove my heels into the sides of his legs to hold myself in place—until we both are spent and panting.

Which, as you would expect from a well-conditioned athlete, takes quite some time.

After a few precious moments of his face snuggled into my hair, he picks me up and carries me into his bedroom.

When he is finished with me and passes out, the sun is peeking over the horizon.

I throw on his shirt, belt it with his tie, slip on my shoes, and then steal the pizza from his fridge on my way to catch a cab.

MISSION: DAY TWO

"HOW'D IT GO?" Ari asks when I arrive back at our hotel suite. He's still wearing his tuxedo, and I suspect he just got in himself.

"If we didn't have a mission, I'd have stayed a few days."

"And you can cross both Olympic athlete and Vice President's son off your sexual bucket list."

"Very funny. That was work. We need to meet the Prince. What did you do?"

"I have my own iron in the fire."

I squint at him. "How so?"

He pulls up his pants and grins.

"You didn't! With Allie?" He shrugs. "You good?"

"You wanna find out?" he replies with a smirk.

"Ew. No, you're supposed to be my brother."

He shrugs. I want to punch him. "I'm just saying, you ever need to blow off some steam, you and I both know we're not really related."

"Did you ever visit Blackwood?"

"No, but I was briefed on your training."

"They told you about my sex life? How in the world—"

"You were under a microscope the entire time you were there. That's pretty obvious from your school file."

"You got to read about me? That isn't fair. I don't know anything about you."

"There wasn't much in it. Just stuff like your grades and how good you are at, well—everything. But it didn't tell me anything about your personal life. What about your family?"

"They're dead."

"How did they die?" he asks.

"I don't want to talk about it."

"Look, I'm not trying to pry—"

I interrupt him. "Why did you get chosen for this mission?"

"Not sure, but I think I'm your babysitter."

"Why would you be that?"

"Maybe because I don't have a vagina of my own, and I look silly in a bikini."

I roll my eyes at him. "You're obnoxious. Can we have this conversation after I've had some sleep?"

"You can sleep on the plane. I just ordered us breakfast."

"How did you know when I'd get here?"

"Because, I think we're a lot alike. That's the goal, right? Leave them wanting more? You had to give Daniel a taste, so he will crave more. The question is, which one of us will win? Shall we wager a bet?"

"So you slept with Allie so she would sleep with Peter and talk him into going to Montrovia? What if she shows up alone? Peter is key to this plan. You better not have screwed that up."

"I was hoping you might be smart and sleep with Peter instead of Daniel."

"Peter isn't really my type, but you're right. We need access to their group of friends if we're going to play this game. They would give us instant legitimacy."

"And a two-pronged approach is always safer than going it alone." He leans around, his eyes lowering to my ass. "I was told to watch your six. Not too bad of a job."

I hold my hand in front of my butt. "Stop that! You can't be lusting after me if we are going to play brother and sister."

"Do you have real brothers and sisters? A family?"

"No. Do you?"

"Not anymore."

"What happened?"

"My mother died of cancer when I was eleven. My

father was a four-star Army general stationed at the Pentagon. He died in a car accident a few years ago." He slides his computer toward me. "Take a look at this. It's our joint bank account."

I blink a few times trying to comprehend what I'm seeing. Finally, I say, "That's a whole lot of zeros."

"And apparently just our slush fund. We have other investments, too. It's crazy."

"Is it real?"

He grins at me. "I say we go shopping in Montrovia and find out."

ROOM SERVICE BRINGS breakfast, but I use the micro-wave to heat up the pizza I stole while Ellis and the Kates oversee the loading of our luggage.

Ari groans when I get in the limo with it. "Oh, that smells horrible."

"It's not. It's amazing."

He holds his head. "I'm fighting a hangover."

"Do you normally drink much? I mean—"

He holds up his hand to silence me. "I don't need the talk, sis. I know what's at stake."

I nod. "Good. So do we have a plan once we get there?"

"I think we're just supposed to get settled in the villa. Go The Casino. Make friends."

"And hopefully the Prince will just show up? No

way. We're going to start with shopping. We're going to spend an obscene amount on a car. We're going to drive it to The Casino, looking fabulous, and we'll get people talking. We're going to gamble like crazy, which means they will start coming to us. Once they do, we throw a party. We have to have a plan B in case our plan A's don't show up. And that includes you getting friendly with the Prince's cousin."

"What does she look like?"

"It doesn't matter. She's next in line to the throne, followed by her younger sister. I mean, think about it. What's the big deal if the Prince is killed? There's a whole line of relatives who would take over. They can't kill them all off."

"I suppose," he says.

"Still it's odd that there was nothing in our dossier about the cousins. I wonder why not?"

"Ask Ellis."

"I will on the plane."

WE GET LOADED on the plane. I bring my pizza box with me, dragging it around like it's Daniel's class ring or something. But I really am enjoying the pizza. And I'm going to have more when I wake up.

But first things first.

"Ellis, what do you know about the Prince's cousins? Why isn't there more on them in our packets?"

"This case is for you to figure out. But I can get you any information you ask for."

"I want everything you can tell me about the next five people in line for the throne. I also want to know how many are in line, and what happens if they reach the end of the line?"

He pecks away at a computer. "There are seventy-two in line."

"Are they all going to be together anytime soon? All in the same place?"

"I would suspect the large majority of them will be at the Queen's Ball which takes place after the race and is the finale for the week."

"So they could take them all out, with a bomb or something? Destroy the castle?" Ari asks. "Who rules then?"

"If that were to happen, the highest ranking military official would take over the country, and his bloodline would become royalty. He wouldn't inherit their money though. The royal family's funds would go to trusts and charities in the case of no blood relatives."

"Do we know anything about the highest ranking military official?" I ask.

"Yes, he's a close friend of the King. Was the best man at his wedding. Very wealthy and ready to retire soon."

"And his second in command?" Ari wonders.

"The Prince's godfather."

"Hmmm. Alright. Let's sleep on it," I suggest. "We need to look fresh for our descent into Montrovian society."

MISSION: DAY THREE

ELLIS WAKES ME up precisely an hour before we are due to land so I can freshen up.

I can barely believe that I just slept for ten hours straight. On a plane. On the way to my first mission.

Note to self: Hot sex is a must before the start of every mission. I close my eyes, allowing myself a moment to relive my night with Daniel. But when I open them back up, I'm all business.

I do my makeup, put on a tight black dress and heels so pointy, I could kill a man with them.

Ari and I don't go to The Casino first thing as we had originally planned. We're too busy checking out our villa.

I didn't expect this. I assumed a villa was a quaint little place—small and cozy.

In Montrovia, villa equals mansion. We're staying in a massive stucco and tile-roofed home with sweeping terraces overlooking the harbor; a private courtyard featuring an amazing pool and a pool house containing a full bar, kitchen, and gaming tables; and a tennis court. Not to mention a garage full of exotic cars. I'd never leave, except I'm dying to drive them all.

I suggest that we take one of the cars and go shopping in town, but Ellis informs me I have someone coming from Tech and can't leave.

Ari decides not to wait for me. He chooses a silver Maserati and backs out of the garage.

TECH EQUALS GADGETS. And every spy should have some of those, right?

And apparently Black X agents are no exception.

After Ari leaves, I'm taken down a hidden elevator in the garage to a large secret room made of concrete and corrugated pipe. The floor is a gorgeous terra cotta tile, and the pipe is painted a soft creamy color. It looks like a cross between a wine cellar and a bomb shelter.

I'm introduced to Terrance. He's young and cute, if not slightly nerdy. He also looks jet lagged.

"You look tired," I say.

"I wasn't exactly prepared for this trip. Someone else was assigned to you, but he got sick."

"With what?"

"Death."

"He's dead? What happened?"

"Massive heart attack, I guess."

I wonder why he doesn't mention Black X.

Either Terrance and Ari don't know about it, or they aren't supposed to talk about it. Maybe I'm not supposed to talk about it either. Terrance takes off his glasses, wipes the lenses with a cloth, and studies me. "You're very young."

"I'm twenty," I say confidently, giving him my cover age and knowing that the clothes and makeup I'm wearing make me look much older than my eighteen years.

"And you trained at The Farm?"

"No. Blackwood Academy."

"Never heard of it. So are you any good?" He shakes his head, talking to himself. "Of course you are. And this must be a very important mission. I was put on a private plane and told to do everything I can to help you. I understand you will be attending numerous social events, so I'm going to fix you up. Let's start with your watch. I'll update it," he says, unclasping it from my wrist.

"Update it?"

"Unless someone already has." He takes out a small tool and pops open the back. "See, the liquid in these darts has turned blue. Blue means it's not as effective. It should be purple."

I want to ask him why the hell my father's watch has darts in it. It takes all my will power to clamp my mouth shut and not let out a big WTF. Was my father a spy?

I nod, playing it cool.

I take a deep breath and assimilate this new information.

My dad was a spy, not the international businessman I thought he was? So why didn't anyone tell me that? Why during all my years at Blackwood didn't anyone mention this fun fact?

Memories of my mom and dad rushing off on business—sometimes separate, sometimes together, and sometimes with me—cloud my vision. I remember simple rules they taught me. *Always sit with your back to the wall. Be aware of your surroundings. Immerse yourself in the region's language and culture. Blend in.*

Our lifestyle and our travel—were mom and I his cover? A man on vacation with his family?

I think about the man who killed my mother. Although I've dreamed about it for years, I've never broken it down. Never used my current knowledge to assess the former situation. Obviously, the man was an assassin.

Could my mother have been a spy, too?

Terrance interrupts my line of thought. "Okay, here's the watch back. Three o'clock is stun. Six o'clock will knock someone out. Nine o'clock gives them a dose of truth serum. Midnight is lethal. Do you know how to fire it?"

I shake my head. "I didn't know the watch did all that."

"That's okay. It's easy." He holds my arm out, shows me how to set the time, how to aim, and how to fire.

"So you're a spy, and your dad is a spy. That's really cool. My dad is a mathematician."

"How old are you?"

"I'm twenty-six."

"How did you get this job?"

"How does anyone get this kind of job? They recruited me. I graduated MIT with a Masters in mathematics and a Doctorate in quantum physics. But they noticed me because I created a bomb the size of a Band-Aid."

"Do I get one of those?"

He pulls a box of pore cleansing strips out of his bag. "Don't use these on your face," he says with a laugh, taking one out of the box and putting it on a sample of cement in the basement. "Peel the back off, stick it to what you want, then you have five seconds to get out of the way."

We move way back as the cement explodes and disintegrates.

"That's pretty slick."

He pulls a syringe out of a container next. "Give me your arm."

"For what?"

"I'm supposed to inject you with a tracking device. It's for your own safety."

"I'm not cool with that," I tell him. "Is it optional?"

"I was told you were to have one, if that's what you're asking. I need to follow my orders."

"Do *you* have one?"

"No freaking way. That stuff can be hacked into . . ." He stops talking. "Shit."

"I'd like to decline."

"I'll say I forgot. That your beauty got me all flustered." He blushes. "Give me your phone."

I do, and he adds a couple apps to it. One that allows me to eavesdrop on nearby conversations and another that picks up GPS signals from the trackers he's going to show me later.

"What else do you have for me?" I ask.

He takes a ring out. "I retrofitted this on the flight here. It's a black diamond. Very expensive, very rare. If you do this," he takes my hand in his and slams it down on the table, "a spike comes out of the setting. Very small. Very deadly. One little prick of it will immediately cause paralysis and then death. I'd suggest using an uppercut to the chin to administer it."

I nod. "Got it."

"Take off your shoes and leave them with me." He pulls a pair of gorgeous black studded Louboutins out of his bag. As I slide them on my feet, he says, "I will be down here for a few hours until all your shoes are complete. Each one will have a knife hidden in the left toe. Click your heel on a hard surface to pop it out."

I click the heel and out pops a pointed blade. "How do I get it back inside?"

"Click the heel again." I do so, and the blade disappears. "Nice. How do you come up with all of this?"

"It's what they pay me for. Although, I will admit, this is the first time I've ever done heels like these. I tried to read up on you. You don't have a file."

"I'm undercover. A file would kind of defeat the purpose."

"Every spy, no matter how dark, has some kind of internal file," he insists, then goes on to show me more gadgets. A lipstick video camera, dot-style candies that are really real-time GPS tracking devices, a nail polish that will dissolve metal, and dental floss that is a high-tenacity wire that I could use to either kill a man or rappel down the side of a building.

While he's been showing me everything, I've been thinking about my parents. Specifically about what my mother pulled off her neck and shoved into my hand when she told me to stay hidden in the closet and not come out no matter what I heard. She told me it was *top secret*. I assumed she meant that I wasn't supposed to tell anyone about it—and I haven't. But now I wonder if top secret meant it contained top secret information.

Something worth dying for.

I pull the locket from around my neck. I've kept it hidden all these years but decided to wear it on my first mission.

"Could you update this, too?" I ask, knowing I'm taking a big risk.

He studies the locket. "Hmm, click the top once to take a photo, right?"

I nod, even though I haven't got a clue.

He gets his magnifying glasses back out and takes the locket completely apart. "So your parents were both spies? How cool is that?"

"Well, they're both dead, so . . ."

"I'm sorry." He fumbles the locket. "If they were killed, why do you want to follow in their footsteps?"

"Did they not brief you on me?"

"No. I told you, I was a last minute addition to the team. Not much time for prep."

He gets the locket open, pulls out a tiny computer disk, and hands it to me. "Do you know what's on this?"

"Just a bunch of selfies," I lie. "I realized they aren't that fun to take when you can't see the results right away."

He chuckles. "You can go on your shopping spree now."

"Thanks for everything, Terrance," I say, giving him a quick peck on the cheek that causes him to blush again.

"You're welcome," he says, shaking my hand as I get in the elevator.

Once I'm out of the garage and on Cap's glitzy main street, I open my fist and read the piece of paper Terrance put into my hand.

I don't know who you are working for, but your entire villa—minus the basement—is wired. Be careful.

And I believe him.

Especially after learning my parents were spies.

How do I trust anyone when they didn't trust me enough to tell me the truth?

I CALL ARI to find out where he is and meet him at a designer store, where he's doing exactly what we said we'd do when we got here—spending a boatload of cash.

"That suit looks good on you," I tell him, admiring his tall frame in a black Prada tuxedo.

A salesgirl is fawning over him. "I told you that cut was perfect on you. It barely needs tailoring."

"We're going to The Casino tonight. My sister needs an amazing dress. Where would you suggest she go?"

"We have a large collection of couture evening wear just next door. Would you like me to escort her there?"

"Yes, please," Ari says. "We don't want her getting into too much trouble along the way."

I roll my eyes at him and say to the salesgirl, "Just point me in the right direction. I'll find my way later.

What all did you get, Ari?"

"A couple dozen suits and shirts. Pick me out some ties. And, I know, I just bought a new wardrobe in D.C., but the climate here really requires a different weight of fabric."

The salesgirl is nodding in agreement and probably already knows how she's going to spend her commission.

I smile at Ari. For a guy who claims to not like shopping, he is playing his role well.

I wander around looking at ties. The store isn't very busy. They say most people who come to experience Race Week arrive today or tomorrow, hitting the extravagant restaurants, casino, and clubs before the special events start later in the week. I'm holding up a tie to one of the suits Ari purchased when two men come through the back door. The first man is the Prince of Montrovia's bodyguard, and the second is none other than his Royal Highness. I pretend not to notice, turning my back to them and studying the tie, then comparing it to another.

"I like the blue one the best," a sultry voice with a sexy accent says.

I glance over my shoulder and gaze into the Prince's dark eyes. "I was thinking the blue was a little boring."

"Too traditional?" he asks.

"Yes, whereas this gold one is a little more exciting. Not to mention it matches one of his cars."

"And what kind of car is that?"

"A Lamborghini Aventador."

"And it's gold?"

"Gold plated. Purchased from some spoiled prince somewhere."

"Will it be in the car show?"

"I don't think so. I mean, he'll probably drive it there. It's our first time here for the car show. I'm not really sure how it all works." I tilt my head toward him and whisper, "Honestly, the car is a little flashy for my taste."

The Prince smiles, leaning in close to me and whispering back, "What kind of cars do you like?"

"Fast ones."

"I like fast things, too," he says, giving me a once over. "Have you driven any fast ones?"

"I have a new car that just arrived in Montrovia, but I haven't had the chance to get her out of the garage yet."

"Let me guess. You would look good in something red. A Ferrari convertible, perhaps?"

"Hmmm. Afraid not. I prefer something a little more, um, challenging. Thanks for your input on the tie. I'll be sure to tell my brother the Prince of Montrovia prefers traditional things." He looks surprised. "What, did you think that if you came in the back door no one would recognize you? Have a good day, your Royal Highness."

I take both ties over to the salesgirl and tell her to let Ari know that I'll be next door trying on gowns—and I say it loudly enough for the Prince to overhear.

I'M IN FRONT of the mirror checking out the third gown I've tried on—a gorgeous gilded Atelier Versace—when the Prince strolls over and says, "That looks lovely on you."

"Thank you."

"Will you be at The Royal Montrovian Casino tonight?"

"We're told it's the place to be."

He holds out two tickets. "I'm having a private party. You should wear that dress. And please, allow me to introduce myself. I'm Lorenzo Vallenta." He holds out his hand for me to shake, but when I place my hand in his, he turns it over and kisses it. "And what is your name?"

"I'm Huntley Von Allister."

"Huntley. It's a pleasure to meet you."

"Thanks."

The Prince narrows his eyes at me. "Will you be there?"

"At your party?"

"Yes."

"Maybe. But I probably won't be wearing this dress."

"What will you be wearing?" he asks, truly looking

confused. I'm pretty sure no woman has ever RSVP'd *maybe* to a personal invite from him.

"What I'm wearing is a surprise," I reply, purposefully playing coy.

BACK AT HOME, I show Ari the tickets. He's thrilled and, of course, wants to go.

"I don't think that should be our game plan. The Prince is used to women fawning over him. A man like him needs a challenge to stay interested. He must believe I'm *not* interested."

"Women," Ari mutters, but nods his head in agreement. "So I thought we'd do dinner and then go to The Casino. Sound good?"

"Yes. We need to make friends."

"Ellis booked us a table at—and I quote—*the first hotel restaurant ever to be awarded three Michelin Stars, which it has never since lost.* The ambiance is supposed to be incredible," he says, flashing me a pic of the restaurant on his phone.

"Hmm," I say. "What do you think? It doesn't look like a place to meet people."

"You're right. It looks really stuffy." He does a quick Internet search and comes up with a better option. "How about this place, instead? It says that its dining experience is enhanced due to an open kitchen and an elaborate counter around which we can dine."

"I think it would be easier to meet people there. It looks fun."

He reads more. "It also has an incredible view of the harbor, and it has one Michelin Star after only being open for three years. So, the food must be good. Alright. I'll have Ellis get us in."

Ellis walks into the room, bringing us each a flute of champagne.

After Ari asks him to change our dinner plans, Ellis informs us that our team has intercepted more Internet chatter, and they fully expect an assassination attempt on the Prince during Race Week.

"Was there any indication it would be hidden in a terrorist attack?" Ari inquires. "We discussed the possibility of a bomb at the Queen's Ball."

"No word on that. I'll let you know if I hear anything else." He turns to me. "We have hair and makeup specialists as part of our villa rental along with the housekeeping and kitchen staff. Would you like me to send them to your suite?"

"Yes, thank you. And I think Ari should get his hair done, too."

Ari scowls, almost offended, but he quickly hides it. "I agree," he says.

"I'd like to take a quick nap then get ready. If The Casino and clubs are as big of a deal as I've read about, people will have a late dinner then go there. Let's plan to leave in three hours."

Ari nods in agreement, looking like he could use a nap, too. This is a lot to deal with in a short amount of time.

Well, at least it is for me. Not only do I have to be on point with my new identity and mission, I just found out that my parents were spies and that I am probably in possession of top secret information.

I think about the note Terrance gave me. That I'm being watched by someone. More than likely that includes the keystrokes on the computer I was supplied with. If I'm going to find out what's on that disc, I'm going to have to be careful.

I go to my room, lie down on my bed, set my alarm, and drift off while trying to come up with a plan.

AT DINNER, ARI and I are seated next to four rowdy British lads in town for the race, the cars, and the women. It appears everyone parties all night, sleeps until early afternoon, then does it all over again.

We become fast friends during our meal, and by the end we've moved past small talk.

"It's our fifth year here," one of them tells us. "We started coming when we were still chums at Oxford."

"It's our first time," I admit. "What do I need to know? Like where should we go tonight?"

One of the chums raises his hand. "We volunteer to

show you the ropes."

It doesn't hurt that I'm in a killer dress. Well, pieces of a dress.

Ari rolls his eyes at me. "I thought you were going to the Prince's party tonight." He says to them, "She got tickets today."

"Bollocks," one says.

"Boring," one adds.

Another makes a snoring sound.

I pretend to look perplexed. "I would think there would be a lot of attractive women there."

"Yes, but who all want to be a princess. We prefer to slum in The Casino."

"I doubt anyone slums here," Ari jokes.

"The Prince's parties are small, elite, well-mannered affairs," a tall red head who reminds me of a Weasley informs us.

"And you boys aren't well-mannered?" I ask.

He grins. "We most definitely are not."

The others protest, calling their friend a cad.

Ari continues, still questioning my judgment on this. "But I thought my sister *wanted* to meet the Prince?"

I shrug, like whatever.

"Do you gamble?" the redhead asks.

"I read up on how to play Roulette. I'd like to try that."

"Which one? The English, American, or European

French version?" the tall, good-looking guy named Wesley asks. He's the cutest one of the bunch and my target for tonight.

"No offense to the British," I say, holding up my hands, "but I'd like to play the European French version."

The boys boo.

"Well, let's finish our pints and go then, shall we?" the redhead asks.

"Sounds good to me," Ari replies.

"Would you like a ride?" I ask the group as we depart the restaurant to find Ellis holding open the door to our limo.

"It's just a short walk," one of the guys argues.

"You wouldn't say that if you were wearing these." I pull the hem of my skirt up and show them my sky-high heels.

"Those look like they could kill a man," Wesley teases.

You have no idea.

I grab Wesley's hand and pull him into the limo with me. He's loud, obnoxious, and a flirt, which fits right into my plan to get the Prince's attention.

Because I *won't* be going to his party.

The Casino is loaded with surveillance cameras, and although it is owned by a public company, the Montrovian government and the royal family hold the majority interest.

And, I'm hoping the dress I chose for tonight will attract attention—especially with the amount of money I'll be gambling with.

MISSION: DAY FOUR

THE PRINCE WANDERS into the morning room, his usual full English breakfast of sausage, bacon, eggs, broiled tomato, fried potatoes, toast, and strong coffee waiting for him.

"I don't know how you eat all that in the morning," Juan, his bodyguard and head of security detail says, handing him the local newspaper. "Is this her?"

The Prince studies the photo. Clearly, it's her, and clearly, she is beautiful. And that dress. He reads the caption: *Huntley Von Allister dazzles in a pink gown with an open midriff from the Michael Kors Collection.*

The gown, if you can technically call it that, features a long skirt slung low on her hips in a glittering pink fabric. A matching band of fabric covers her breasts and another circles her neck.

"So, she was at The Casino but didn't come to my party?" the Prince asks, looking bewildered.

"Apparently so, sir. If it's any consolation, her brother showed up."

"Why didn't she?"

"I'm told it's because she was winning an obscene amount at the roulette table."

"Which kind?"

"French European. She garnered a fair amount of attention from Casino security." He tosses a stack of photos at the Prince.

"I'll bet she did." He rifles through them. "She's beaming, gorgeous, and looks fiercely competitive. You can see the seriousness in her eyes. The security camera was positioned as such to take beautiful photos of her." Towards the end of the stack, he notices a tall, good-looking man kissing her in celebration.

Then escorting her out of The Casino, they leave together.

He lays the photos down with a bit of a huff. "Who is the guy?"

"Wesley Windsor, British playboy."

"Royal?"

Juan looks at his notes. "Seventeenth in line for the throne. Grandson of the Queen's daughter."

He studies the photos some more. "It's almost as if she knew where the cameras were and knew I would see these photographs."

Juan chuckles. "Just for you, huh? The photos were made from the surveillance videos."

"Can I please get a Bloody Mary?" the Prince says, causing a staff member to scurry away.

"Hangover, sir? You'd think by now you would have learned," Juan teases.

"Merda."

"Now now, Lorenzo," the Queen scolds, joining the pair at the table. She picks up a photo. "Very pretty. Is she a suspected terrorist or something?"

"Why would you think that?" Lorenzo asks.

"There are an *awful* lot of photos of one girl." His mother laughs. "Although, she does look pretty spectacular in that dress."

Juan replies with a grin. "Well, we can't be too careful, Your Highness. You know the chatter our clandestine forces have been hearing."

"You'd think they'd have better things to do than research a pretty girl who looks harmless."

"If you were trying to kill your son, wouldn't you hire someone who looks like she does to do it?"

The Queen shakes her head. "An assassin wouldn't wear pink." She looks closer and tilts her head. "I've seen this girl before. Just the other day. Where was it?" She taps her finger against her chin, thinking. "I know," she says, grabbing her iPad and typing. "Here it is!" She turns the screen toward the Prince.

He sees another photo of Huntley Von Allister looking stunning, wearing a red gown and dancing with someone he knows.

I WAKE UP to the sounds of the ocean only to have it be overrun with rap music—a loud, angry Detroit version—blaring from the courtyard.

I step out onto the Juliet balcony that overlooks the villa's courtyard and see Ari shirtless by the pool, doing yoga. I study his form as he calmly holds a plank pose, his muscles tight for a long while before his arms finally start to shake. He holds the pose for a few more beats then pops up, sprints across the courtyard, and beats the crap out of a portable punching bag—his odd workout a combination of zen and badass.

I study my brother some more. I was right. He's fully fit, toned, and perfectly muscled. He should be shirtless more often.

I close the door, shutting out the noise, and walk out into the living portion of my suite to find the file I asked for yesterday on my table along with a continental breakfast.

I pluck up the file, pour myself a glass of orange juice, wrap a napkin around a chocolate croissant, and make my way out to the veranda overlooking the Montrovian Harbor.

I savor a bite of the croissant before opening the folder. Inside I find just a single sheet of paper.

Aristotle, or Ari, is apparently his real name. Real last name: Bradford.

Mother passed away from breast cancer. Father was a four-star general stationed at the Pentagon, who died in a traffic accident. Ari went to military school, where they discovered talents in weaponry and hand-to-hand combat. He holds the school's long-range sniper record and was their boxing champion.

I can see why they chose him for this mission. Not only is he qualified, but with his family all gone, it would be easy to change his birth records and create adoption papers. And wham, bam, Ari is the long lost son of a billionaire.

I turn the sheet of paper over, where Ellis has added a handwritten note.

Six months ago, Ari was pulled from his elite school and trained as a covert agent.

Which I find interesting. CIA training is typically a year-long program and for those who are at least twenty-six years old.

I'm distracted from the brief when a text pops up on my phone.

AirForceTwo: *You owe me a pizza . . . and a shirt.*

I look down at my choice of pajamas and smile. But I don't reply. If Daniel wants his shirt back, he'll have to come to Montrovia and get it. I glance at the clock, knowing I need to work out and then get ready for the pool party Ari and I are having today.

Apparently, when you win big at the roulette table in a barely-there dress and have a smoking hot brother, everyone wants to be your friend.

"LOOKS LIKE YOU win," Ari says, elbowing me and nodding toward the entrance to the courtyard.

"Well, isn't this a precarious situation? My hot-as-hell hookup hands me the Prince on a silver platter. I couldn't have planned it better if I had planned it." I elbow Ari back. "Oh wait, I did."

I watch as Daniel enters the courtyard with the Prince of Montrovia. Next to the Prince is a man with a discreet earbud and alert eyes. He's the same guard who was with the Prince in the clothing store. I'm sure the outside of the villa is surrounded by agents, but the fact that there is only one in here is the first flaw I see in his security protocol.

The Prince doesn't approach me right away. He's too busy being swarmed by people who either know him or want to.

Daniel, on the other hand, walks straight over to me. I'm dressed in a bikini, but the way he looks at me makes me feel like I'm standing here naked.

"You crashing my party?" I ask, folding my arms across my chest like I'm mad at him for being here.

"You wanted me to come," he fires back, then kisses both my cheeks. "And, now, here I am. With the Prince, who if I recall, you didn't think I really knew."

"So you flew all the way here just to prove a point?"

"Actually, Lorenzo called and asked about you."

"Why?"

"Apparently, he invited you to his party last night, and you didn't show. Not many women will turn down an invitation from the Prince. You've perplexed the poor guy." Daniel laughs. I can tell he finds my not going to the party humorous.

"That wasn't my intention. I just happened to be busy."

"Doing what? Or should I say, *whom*?"

"What do you mean?"

He flashes a photo of Wesley and me leaving The Casino last night.

"That's none of your business," I say.

"Dang. I was going to compare battle wounds with him."

"What are you talking about?"

He points down to his calves, which are indeed boasting fresh red tracks down the outsides. "Your sexy heels almost ruined my photogenic-ness—my perfect specimen of a body. And the salt water in the pool stung the hell out them." He smirks. "But at least the pain stopped the tears of being ditched in the morning."

"I tried to wake you up."

"You did not. The shirt isn't that big of deal, but stealing a man's breakfast pizza? That was just cold." I get the dimple. "Oh, look. Lorenzo is working his way over here. You should cover up. That bikini is practically obscene."

I punch him in the arm. "It is not."

He whispers, "It's sexy as hell. Maybe I just don't want the Prince seeing you like that. Really, I don't want anyone seeing you like that. Want to borrow my shirt?" He pulls his shirt off, revealing his muscular chest and tight abs. I want to run my fingers across them.

So I do.

"Tease," he says, grabbing my hands and giving me another blink of a dimple. God, I love the way he smiles. I fight the urge to grab his face and start making out with him, but I'm on a mission and although I want the Prince to have to work for it a little, I don't want to run him off when I'm this close.

Daniel turns toward the Prince. "Lorenzo, this is my friend, Huntley. We met a few days ago at an event in D.C., and when I mentioned I knew you, she didn't believe me."

"That's not exactly right," I contradict. "He was

bragging about knowing you, so I rolled my eyes. Which he assumed was me not believing him and took it as a challenge, rather than accepting it for what it really was—me not being impressed."

The Prince chuckles, which is good.

"It's nice to see you again," I say to the Prince. "Am I supposed to bow or something?"

"Only to my father, the King."

Daniel laughs and points a finger at him. "He must like you, cuz he makes *lots* of girls kneel."

To prove his point, a girl interrupts us, getting on her knees and lowering her head straight toward the Prince's royal privates.

When she gets up, she whispers something in his ear, presumably about how she's available even though she introduced me to her boyfriend earlier.

But, based on how close she was allowed to get to him without thought shows another flaw in his security. Women aren't viewed as a threat.

"Cool party trick," I say as the girl leaves. "So why are you two really here?"

The Prince throws his thumb in Daniel's direction. "He says you owe him a pizza."

I hold a finger up, causing a steward to instantly appear at my side. I whisper something to him and a few seconds later he presents Daniel with a box.

"What is this?" he asks.

I lean toward the Prince and pretend to confide in him. "It's my new favorite combination, so I ordered it for our party."

Daniel opens the box, looking confused, but the pizza quickly steals his attention. He offers the Prince a piece, but the Prince turns up his nose, takes my elbow, and leads me away from the crowd. I notice his security does not follow.

He kisses my hand. "It's nice to see you again. I had hoped to see you at my party last night."

"Oh, sorry. I got caught up at the roulette table."

"Was your luck good?"

"It was very good."

"Congratulations." He looks back at Daniel. "I can see why Daniel wanted to come to your party. You are very beautiful."

"Thank you. But I doubt he came here for me. Isn't Montrovia where all the rich playboy types will be this week?"

"Possibly. Regardless, I'm glad he allowed me to join him."

"I will admit, it's not every day that a Prince crashes your party."

"So, what brings you to my fair country?" His gaze is intense. I like it. He actually seems interested in talking to me. It's a refreshing change of pace from the guys at Blackwood who just wanted to hookup.

"Same as everyone. The race."

"Would you do me the honor of coming to my party, since I crashed yours?"

"When is it?"

"Well, my party lasts all week."

"When ever will you sleep?" I flirt. The Prince is holding back a smirk. I narrow my eyes at him. "Lorenzo, are you thinking of us together in bed?"

"Perhaps," he says, not admitting a thing. Then he adds, "Trust me, there is plenty of time for pleasure between parties. It's a week full of special events."

"I know. We got tickets for the race and the car show."

"There are events nearly every day and night this week. My private yacht is the best place to view the race, and we end the festivities with the Queen's Ball. Girls from all over the world hope to be my date."

"It must suck to be the Prince."

He's taken aback. "That's not the reaction I usually get. Why do you say that?"

"I suspect it's like a buffet—so many options that you can't choose just one."

"Are you saying you don't want to be my date?" He looks confused. I think Daniel is right. I don't think he's ever been turned down before.

"No offense, but I wasn't one of those little girls who dreamed of becoming a princess."

"Too bad. You're breathtaking," the Prince says, touching my face.

"Thanks," I say awkwardly, mostly because no one has ever said that to me before.

He stares into my eyes, his hand on my face. "We're causing a bit of a scene."

I look around—even though I am fully aware of what is going on around me. Mostly. I had to let my guard down for a few minutes to focus on the Prince—and only him—to make him feel like the only man in the room.

"How are we causing a scene? We're talking."

"You're new in town and have held my attention longer than most of my dates."

"Yay for me!"

"Sarcasm. I like it," he says, flashing a conspiratorial grin.

"I'll just tell everyone that I was standing close to you because you smell good." I will admit, so far, I actually like the Prince. He's clearly trying to impress me. He's charming, polite, has a sexy-as-hell accent, and does smell quite intoxicating.

He touches the tip of my nose. "You're cute."

I say, "Thank you, Your Highness," in Montrovian.

He cocks his head in surprise. "You speak our language?"

"A little. I have an affinity for languages."

"Not many people speak our native tongue anymore."

"I know. I'm kind of a history buff," I say.

"My country has a great many historical sites."

"I know that, too. My brother may have come for the cars, but I came for the history. While he's sleeping off last night, I'll be visiting the art museum, the hot springs, and going on a tour of the castle."

"The castle? Well, you know most of the rooms aren't included in the public tour. You'd need to know someone if you wanted to see the best parts."

I sigh and roll my eyes. "Let me guess. The best part is *your* place?"

He laughs. "I'd show you the rest of the castle, too. Would you like a private tour?"

"I'd love that, actually."

"I will send my driver for you tomorrow at noon."

"No."

"But you just said you wanted—"

"You aren't sending your driver. If you wanna hang out with me, you can come get me yourself. Or I'll drive."

"You did mention that you have a new car here. Care to drive me home?"

"Sure, why not?" I smile as I escort him down to the garage.

He whistles at the car I've been dying to get behind

the wheel of and says, "This isn't a street car, it's a track car."

I don't know who was in charge of acquiring this car, but they get two big thumbs up from me. "I'm pretty sure it's street legal. Besides, I'm with the Prince of Montrovia, I should be able to drive whatever I want, don't you think?"

"This car is amazing. I've never seen anything like it."

"That's because there were only two made. They had planned to make three, but the white carbon fiber proved to be difficult, so they only made two. It's a Koenigsegg CCXR Trevita. Bad ass, right?"

"I'll say. How did you get it?"

"I recently came into some money." He raises his eyebrow at me, and then looks at the car again. "Well," I clarify, "it was quite a lot of money."

"Roulette?" he laughs.

I lower my eyes and my voice. "My father passed away."

He touches my hand gently. "My own father is gravely ill. It's only a matter of time."

"Are you spending a lot of time with him?"

"Not as much as I'd like."

"You should make the time. Even if it's hard. My dad died suddenly. Massive heart attack."

"But he didn't suffer. It's hard to watch your father,

the King, a man who has always been larger than life, wither away."

"I suppose, but trust me, you should be with him. Every day."

"Will you come with me?" he asks with such emotion I have no other possible answer.

"Yes."

"Maybe it will help you heal too, no?"

"Maybe. I didn't know my father. My parents passed away when I was younger, and I recently got a call from an attorney asking me to come for the reading of a will. There, I discovered who my real father was and that I also have a brother. We are taking some time off to travel together. See the world. Get to know each other. Ari lost his parents too, so we're the only family each other has."

I'm surprised when he wraps me in a hug. "So much tragedy for someone so young."

I allow him to console me. It's really sweet.

"So are you ready to go for a ride?"

"Oh, I think so."

We get buckled up and pull out of the drive. I take it easy through the city streets, giving people plenty of time to gawk at the car and take photos.

Ten minutes later, we're winding up the hill to the castle and pulling through the gates. I take in my surroundings like I was trained to do.

"You have an airstrip up here."

"Yes, for landing smaller planes."

"Anyone planning on using it in the next few minutes?"

"I don't believe so, why are you asking?"

I throw the car in neutral, rev the motor, and raise my eyebrows at him. "What do you say? I would love to see what she can do, and everything in Montrovia is really cliffy."

"Cliffy?" He laughs. "Does that mean what I think?"

"What do you think it means?"

He gives me a smirk, shrugs his shoulders, and turns his hands sideways gesturing down at his pants.

"Cliffy? As in your hard dick?" I ask, stifling a laugh.

He bites his lip, a little embarrassed. It's sexy as hell.

"Cliffy means that the roads are all on cliffs, and I don't want to drive off one of them and splat into the Med. What you are referring to is a stiffy. A boner. Hot. Hard. Ready for action."

"Oh, yes, stiff. That would make sense."

I drive to the end of the runway. "You ready for this?"

He doesn't get a chance to respond because I quickly rev the engine and drop the hammer. The tires scream for every ounce of grip they can find. I use the paddle shifters to switch gears, the car responding effortlessly. This car is stupid fast and since it has a super charger as opposed to a turbo, there isn't the kick every time I shift.

The car just rockets down the runway.

"How fast are you going?" the Prince yells. "Slow down."

"I read you race for fun. You should be used to this."

"There's a difference. I'm not driving. A girl is."

When I reach the other end of the runway—which happens quickly—I slam on the brakes, downshift, and swing the car around ninety degrees to prove a point, then hit the throttle again.

"What the hell are you doing?" he asks, looking very nervous.

"We haven't even hit top speed yet, but we're going to try."

"What's her top speed?"

"Four hundred and ten kilometers per hour. That's like triple the speed limit in America." I push the car, finally getting it up to four hundred, before I have to stop at the other end of the runway. "Holy shit. Wasn't that fun?"

"Why do I get the feeling you aren't just here for the history?"

"Okay, so maybe I like the cars, too. What do you say? Wanna do it again?"

"Only if I can drive." He starts laughing then he sobers. "Actually, I have a better idea."

He instructs me to pull around the castle and out onto the lawn.

"Am I going to get in trouble for this?" I ask.

"Just the opposite," he says. "My father loves cars. If he's having a good day, he might be able to come out and see it."

What he says touches my heart.

I use the hydraulics to lift the chassis so its profile is not as low and, hopefully, I'm not getting grass all up in the grill.

We enter the castle through a set of French doors that lead directly to the King's suite. I know I'm with the Prince and that we checked in at the gates, but this seems way too easy. I could take out both the King and the Prince in less than a minute if I were playing for the other team.

The King looks very tired, but his face lights up when he sees his son. "Lorenzo!" he exclaims.

"Hello, Papa, how are you feeling today? I brought a friend for you to meet, and we have a surprise for you."

"Are you getting married?" he asks.

The Prince blushes. "No, we have just met, but I am hoping she will accompany me to the events this week."

"Including the Queen's Ball?"

"Um, yes. Except I haven't formally asked her yet." He turns toward me and holds out his hand. I take it and allow him to lead me toward the bed. "I'd like you to meet Huntley Von Allister."

"Von Allister? As in Ares Von Allister?"

"Yes, he was my father. Did you know him?"

"A long time ago, yes. When we were young men. How is he?"

"He passed away a few weeks ago."

The King is somber as he reaches for my hand. "I'm sorry for your loss. He was an interesting man. Smart as hell. And you are quite beautiful. I can see why my son fancies you."

"Thank you, Your Highness. But I think Lorenzo might fancy my car a bit more than me."

"Your car?"

I smile. "He had me pull it up to your terrace so that you could come out and see it."

"What kind of car is it?"

"A Koenigsegg. One of only two produced. Prior to this car, they only had access to a traditional black carbon fiber, but this one is white."

"White?"

"Yes, a silvery, sparkling white that looks like millions of diamonds when the sunlight hits it."

The King smiles and sits up. "This I must see." He looks over at a nurse. "Can we unhook this thing?"

"Yes, of course," the nurse says, undoing the IV.

"I haven't had a proper stroll in a few days."

"Huntley, why don't you lead the way?" Lorenzo suggests, so I walk slowly toward the doors, suddenly realizing how few clothes I have on. I only threw a short cover-up over my bikini when I took the Prince to see my car.

I turn around and notice both the men are following me with grins on their faces. I'm not sure if it's from seeing my backside or the excitement of the car, but whichever works. The King looks happy.

"Wow, now that's a car," the King says. "Tell me about it."

"Koenigsegg aluminum V8, double overhead camshafts. Zero to 100 kilometers per hour in 2.9 seconds. Top speed of over 410. The fuel tanks are integrated for optimal weight distribution and safety, and it even has a detachable hardtop."

The King moves around the car. "The color is stunning. Will this be in the auto show?"

I shake my head.

"You must remedy that, Lorenzo," he says.

"Yes, I must."

His father seems to tire quickly, so we escort him back inside and say goodbye.

"Thank you for making my day," the King says, giving me a wink. "And try to keep him out of mischief."

"I'm probably the wrong girl for that job," I tease.

The Prince takes my hand and leads me into the castle's hallway. It has a magnificent hand-painted, barreled ceiling set atop massive stained-glassed windows.

"This hallway alone is worth the price of admission."

"This hallway isn't on the tour. It's part of my parents' residence." He pulls me into his arms. "Thank you for that. For being so kind to my father."

"You're welcome."

"My one regret is that my father won't get to see me marry. I have spent too much time behaving like a boy. If I don't choose a wife by my twenty-sixth birthday, then one will be chosen for me. My father worries my playboy ways mean I'm not mature enough to rule."

"Doesn't Parliament rule?"

"The answer to that is, sort of. The parliament oversees the day-to-day operations of the country, but the King rules and controls the military. I had to do a stint with our Royal Maritime Division."

At least he's not a wimp who can't take care of himself.

He brings his lips to mine in a soft kiss and murmurs, "Would you like to be my princess?"

I back away, rolling my eyes. "Does that usually work?"

"What ever do you mean?"

"I suppose dangling jewels in front of every girl you bed would get expensive, but the promise of being a princess—that's cheap."

"Are you saying I'm cheap?"

"I'm saying you'll say anything to get a woman into bed."

"Sweetheart, we both know all I have to say is that I'm a prince, and they spread their legs willingly. Honestly, it gets a little tedious. I get the feeling you aren't interested in me."

I let out a laugh. "So, of course, that makes you want me. Princes are probably used to getting everything they want."

"Shall we test that theory in my bedroom? I can make it the next stop on our tour," he says, raising a dark eyebrow in my direction.

"No." It's obvious that the only way I'm going to keep his attention is by pretending not to be interested. He takes my hand, undeterred.

"See, I don't get everything I want. Are you spoken for?"

"No."

"Are you sleeping with Daniel?"

"No comment."

"So, you do sleep around?"

"Sometimes, if the mood strikes me. But I'd prefer romance on the path to love."

"I can do romance," he says, stealing another kiss.

"Your accent is sexy as hell."

"*All* of me is sexy as hell, but I'll let you discover that slowly."

"And the promise of a castle tour?"

"Still good. If you will allow me to escort you to the

Queen's Ball."

"I'd be honored."

He holds out his elbow for me. "Then let the tour commence. The hallway you see here is built on the foundation of the original castle built during the height of the Renaissance period by Lorenzo the Magnificent. He was given the country's land by his family and became Duke of Vallenta. His decedents had marriages arranged to royal families from France, Italy, and Spain, keeping the bloodlines of nobility and allowing them to live without war.

"Descendants of the House of Vallenta have ruled from this land since the fifteenth century. The hallway is so ornate because at one time it led from the Court of Honor to the Throne Room. Now, it leads from the King's home, to the Prince's residence, and then beyond to the public areas of the castle."

He takes me through room after room filled with incredible architecture and history.

The library is particularly spectacular—octagonal in shape with stone walls and tall, arched bookcases with thick moldings accented by black onyx.

The Prince pulls out books of ancient poetry and reads them to me.

"Here's a good one by San Agustín," he says, flipping through another. "*La medida del amor es amar sin medida.*"

"The measure of love is to love without measuring," I say, quickly translating. "That's really pretty and—" I stop speaking when gunshots ring out.

"What was that?" The Prince's eyes get big, and he goes rushing toward the door.

I grab his shirt to stop him, quickly transitioning from flirting to readiness while pretending to be nervous. "Where is your guard?"

"I left him at your place. I forgot to tell him we were leaving."

An alarm sounds.

More shots ring out, sounding closer this time.

I don't know what's going on, but we are sitting ducks here in the library. The only way out, besides the two palladium windows, is the long hallway we've been working our way down. I imagine an ops team storming the castle and now sweeping each room in pairs until they find what they want. The good news is I can't smell any kind of poisonous gas, haven't heard any flash bangs, and can't see assault team movement outside the windows.

"What's your security protocol in a time like this?"

"Screw protocol. I need to see what's going on." He tries to shrug me off.

"Don't you watch movies? I'm assuming gun fire is not an everyday occurrence in the castle?"

"Well, no."

"Lorenzo, you're the Prince. It's your responsibility to your country to keep yourself safe."

"How do I know you're not mixed up in whatever this is?"

"Because you'd already be dead."

He nods. "Good point."

His eyes fill with fear. Fear can be paralyzing.

I gently squeeze his hand to calm him. His eyes are moving wildly with every shot that rings out. I remember reading about all the castle's secret passageways.

"When you were little, did anyone tell you where to hide if anything like this ever happened?"

He looks at me with surprise. "Yes, my grandfather, when I was young. I totally forgot about that." He starts to sing. "*The spotted dog is your friend. Wag his tail then go to the end.*"

He grabs my hand and starts to run toward the door. I pull back. "Where is the dog?"

"The War Room down the hall."

The sounds of gunfire get closer.

I immediately pull the Prince away from the door and toward the fireplace, where I push the third fleur de lis—causing a piece of wood paneling to slide open. I pull him into the passage, knowing we don't have much time. He starts to ask me how I knew to do what I just did, but I hold my fingers to his lips as we quickly and quietly make our way to the War Room.

There's a peephole, thankfully, allowing me to see inside. The room appears to be empty.

But I can feel the chaos in the air. As if someone were breathing on the back of my neck. Danger is near.

But it's now or never.

"Can you wag the spotted dog's tail, quickly? Without exposing yourself?"

The Prince nods, reaches out of the passageway, and moves the tail of a hunting dog carved into an ornate piece of art. Another panel within the passageway we are in slides open slowly as the panel to the War Room closes. It's obvious it's rarely used. I take that as a good sign. I also don't remember this being in anything I read, and I'm hoping it's very much a secret.

I hear the sound of boots thumping on the marble floor and then the War Room door bursting open.

The Prince's eyes get huge. I slap my hand across his mouth to make sure he stays silent. If the gunmen were to hear us, all it would take is a machine gun aimed at the wall to take us both out. The only thing between them and us is a thin wooden panel.

Shots are haphazardly fired into the room, so I pull the Prince into the other passageway, relieved to find it made of stone.

While I'm glad the gunmen can't see us, I hate that I can't see them. I feel blind and part of me would rather face them.

However, it's imperative that I get the Prince somewhere safe first.

We move quickly down the passage and cover a good distance.

I stop for a moment to take my phone out, hoping to call for help.

Of course, there are no bars.

The Prince grabs me, pushes me against the wall, and kisses me. I can feel his heart racing. I tilt my face and allow my lips to brush across his. I've studied what stress chemicals do to the body: a heightened state of awareness, the fight or flight instinct, and a rush of adrenaline. The Prince responds as many a man who fears for his life might—who fears this might be the last time he touches a woman. His hands roughly caress the length of my body as he tightens our embrace.

In this moment, he's forgotten he's a Prince in danger and is acting like just a man.

As much as I am enjoying it, I can't acquiesce. I press my palm against his chest and push him away.

"There has to be more to the poem. Where is the end, and what do you do when you get there?"

He bobs his head, and I can tell he's mentally singing the song again. Finally he says, "I'm supposed to sound the alarm."

I have no idea what that means. The last thing I want to do is sound an alarm that will reveal our exact location, but I'll worry about that when we get there. "Then we must go."

I pull on his hand, but he pulls me back to his lips. "I'd rather kiss you."

"Lorenzo, we need to get you somewhere safe."

"Yes. You are right."

We race through the tunnel, for at least half a mile. Most of it downhill. Like we're heading into town.

Before I can stop him, he pulls a string causing a loud shrilling noise.

"What happens when you do that?" I yell.

"I'm not sure," he admits. "I've never done it before."

"Is there more to the poem?"

He nods and recites. "*Sound the alarm. Call up the Core. Help waits beyond the door.*"

"And you have no idea what lies beyond the door?"

"No, but we seem to have gone downhill, toward town."

"Do you have any weapons?"

"No," he says. But I do. I'm wearing my father's watch. "How is it that you are so calm? I'm freaking out."

"We're safe right now, Lorenzo," I say softly.

"This isn't the way I wanted our date to go," he smiles and trails a finger across my lips, his confidence returning, "although, there is some thrill in danger. Our kiss in the tunnel was exquisite."

"And that is apparently why the papers say you are a *daredevil Prince with no regard for his country.*"

He kisses me again. "You're strong under pressure. You'd make a good princess."

"Let's see what's behind the door," I tell him.

I'm not about to let him get shot and ruin my chances of being a part of Black X permanently.

I discreetly turn my watch dial to midnight and stand with my back against the wall.

"Wait. I should go first," he says.

"You're the future King. No way I'm going to risk a whole country hating on me. I'm going first."

I open the door, sweep the room with my eyes, and find that we are safe, inside the bedroom of a home located in town.

He grins. Looks at the bed. Looks at me. Raises his eyebrows. "A bed. How convenient."

I don't bother to reply. I need to sweep the rest of the home.

Once I determine that we are safe and alone, I say, "Now what?"

"I don't know. I need to go back to the castle and check on my parents. I'll make a call." He pulls his phone out of his pocket.

"Don't!" I grab it from his hand, turn it off, take out the SIM card, and smash it into bits. "Sorry, but you can be tracked by that, and we just got you somewhere safe."

"You are very resourceful," he says, curiously.

"Girl Scout." I shrug like this is basic knowledge then use my phone to call Ari, waiting impatiently as the call is routed through an untraceable network.

"Where the hell are you?" Ari yells at me before I can say anything. "There were shots fired at the castle. The Prince is unaccounted for. The Prince's guard is freaking out trying to find him."

"I'm with the Prince."

"Are you secure?"

"Yes. Please let his bodyguard know. Are his parents alright?"

"Yes, they are."

"What happened?"

"Two men apparently were part of a tour group. They broke away and breached a private part of the castle. Had assault weapons. The press was reporting live as they were there doing an interview with the Queen. There are some injuries but no casualties. The guards were wearing Kevlar. That's all I know."

"Thanks, Ari."

"Well?" the Prince says expectantly when I end the call.

"Two men who were part of a tour group got in. Your parents are fine."

"And the assailants?"

"Not sure. But you can use my phone to call and find out."

A MOTORCADE PICKS us up and returns us to the castle, which is bursting at the seams with military.

I'm taken away from the Prince upon arrival and placed in a room by myself. It's a gorgeous room, formerly the Queen's study. I know it contains a secret passageway that leads to the kitchen, should I need to escape. But since there's a guard standing watch at my door, I'm feeling a little like the enemy, rather than the girl who saved the Prince.

I still have my phone, which is dangling from my shoulder in a Dolce & Gabbana chain wallet. I open it, pulling out a pair of earbuds and then hitting the eavesdropping app on my phone, which now allows me to overhear the conversation taking place next door.

"You can't just take off like that!" someone says.

"And you shouldn't allow him out of your sight!" an older voice booms. "*You* weren't doing your job."

"He doesn't allow me inside when he takes women in the bedroom," the man replies curtly. That must be his personal bodyguard.

"Prince Lorenzo, this has to stop. You are going to be the King—God help us—of our great nation. You need to stop putting yourself at risk where women are concerned. Our investigators are researching this girl's background with a fine-toothed comb. I can't help but think she had something to do with this. It's too much of a coincidence."

"She helped me escape," the Prince says.

"And how did she do that?" the deep voice asks, thick with doubt.

The Prince explains that I suggested a passageway.

"How would she even know about them?"

"She's a history buff and had read up on the castle."

"Why was she here with you? Who is she, really?"

"You think she had something to do with this?" the Prince asks.

"Don't you think it's a little odd this girl you just met asks for a tour of the castle and then we are attacked?"

"No, I don't, because she didn't ask for one. She already bought tickets to the public tour. I offered to bring her here."

I hear an audible sigh on the other end. "Lorenzo, women are your weakness. Why don't you run along now while we question her?"

Ooh, I don't know who that guy is, but I don't think he should be talking to the future King that way. Although, I agree with him on all accounts. The Prince's careless ways make him an easy target.

"Why aren't you questioning the men you captured?"

"Because we didn't capture them, we shot them.

They're both dead."

"Then you're not talking to Huntley without me present."

"Very well. Let's go chat with her together."

I quickly close the app, turn on some music, and pretend not to hear them enter.

The Prince touches my shoulder, and I fake a little jump. "Oh, gosh, you scared me." I take out my earbuds and put them away.

The Prince takes my hand, turning me toward a broad-chested man in military shirtsleeves. Based on the stars on his uniform, I'd say he's important. "Huntley, this is General Agueda of the Montrovian army. He would like to ask you a few questions."

"Um, okay. What's up?" I say, while running my free hand through my hair, fluffing it and looking unconcerned.

"How did you end up at the castle today?" he asks.

"Well, my brother and I were having a party at our villa. Daniel and—"

"Daniel?"

"Spear, sir. The Vice President of the United States' son. Anyway, he and the Prince crashed our party, and Daniel introduced us. We talked, had some champagne, he asked what I planned to do during my visit, and I told him about my plans, which included going on the castle tour. He offered to give me a private one."

The man keeps staring at me, so I continue.

"Then I drove us here, got to meet the King and show him my car—oh gosh, tell me my car didn't get shot."

"It did not," he says. "The breach was between the public part of the castle and the Prince's residence."

I already know that based on where the shots were coming from, but I don't say that. That's not something a normal girl would probably know, plus I need intel. "What happened?"

"Let's not worry about that. How is it you met the Prince again?"

"Why does it sound like—wait, you keeping me in this room for the last hour and now the questions. You don't think *I* had anything to do with whatever happened, do you?" I widen my eyes and turn to the Prince. "Does he? Do you? You were going out there! I stopped you!"

I clench my jaw and cross my arms in apparent outrage at my realization, looking pissed and betrayed.

"I'd like to go home now."

"We aren't finished questioning you," the general says.

"Fine. *You* may finish questioning me, but I won't answer another question if I have to look at him while doing so." I nod toward the Prince.

"Huntley, I'm—" the Prince says.

I give him a defiant look and flip him the bird, causing the general to shoo him out of the room.

I'm questioned for another thirty minutes—where I learn nothing new—before I'm allowed to get in my car and drive home.

I PASS THROUGH the gates of the villa and pull the car into the garage, hoping Ari has learned more than I have about the attack.

"Do you know anything?" I ask, plopping down on the couch, happy to see that the news of the assault on the castle caused the party to dwindle down to nothing.

"Only what we have learned on the news, which isn't much. You were there, what happened?"

"Two gunmen with automatic weapons entered the hallway that connects to the Prince's residence. They were moving down the hall, room by room from the sound of it, in a very military fashion."

"Do we know where they are holding them?"

"At the morgue, I assume. They're dead."

"How do you know that?"

I hold up my phone. "Eavesdropping app."

"So now what?"

"I think we talk about the Prince. He's reckless. His bodyguard does whatever the Prince tells him to do, whether or not it's in his best interest. I didn't study up on the Palace Guard, but the fact that the gunmen were able to get inside the castle is pretty concerning, but then again, I drove in with the Prince, and no one checked me or my car for bombs or weapons. Once inside, I had free run of the place."

"That is concerning," Ari agrees. "We're just going to have to stay close in order to protect him. I really thought any attempt on his life would happen during an outside event."

"Do you think they planned to shoot him or kidnap him?"

"What makes you ask that?"

"I can't imagine what their escape plan would have been for a kidnapping," I say.

"Maybe they knew it was a suicide mission. If a terror organization is behind this, that would make sense."

"Or maybe they knew about the passageways and assumed, like I did, there was a secret one only the Prince would know about."

"Why would they want to kidnap him though? That doesn't make sense. I think they were there to kill."

"I don't know. Control him. Threaten him. Make him do what they want," I suggest.

"Or maybe this was a dry run to see how far they could get. It's not like the Montrovian Guard's protocol is on the Internet like our Secret Service's is."

"A dry run for what exactly?" I ask.

"Maybe they were looking for a place to plant a

bomb. The Queen's Ball is the week's big finale. Remember we talked about a bomb as a possible way to take out most of the Montrovian heirs to the throne?"

"I don't know," I disagree. "We were told the threat was specific to the Prince."

Ellis joins us, bringing a decanter of water and a tray of sandwiches.

"What I wouldn't give for a Jersey Mike's right now," Ari says.

"What is that?" Ellis asks.

"The most amazing sub sandwich you have ever tasted. I get the Giant, over a foot long full of turkey and provolone and done up Mike's way with onions, lettuce, tomatoes, olive oil, red wine vinegar, and spices. It's heaven on bread."

Ellis points at the tray of petite, crustless finger sandwiches. "This will have to suffice for now." He hands me a note then leaves the room.

There is just one sentence inside the note, which I read to Ari. "*Intelligence chatter regarding crown. Keyword: Terra.*"

"What's Terra?" Ari asks.

"I don't know what this is referring to, but Terra was the Roman Goddess of the Earth. In renditions of her, she is always beautiful and usually surrounded by a cornucopia, flowers, and fruit. Sometimes, she is depicted pregnant because she is also the guardian of fertility and motherhood. In planetary science, Terra is the third planet usually referred to as Earth. The male counterpart is Tellus. He was an Athenian statesman in Herodotus's Histories, where he is said to be the happiest man ever because he had a good life and children who remembered him. Apparently, to the ancient Greeks this was the most honorable life. If I remember right, though, he died in a battle, but not before crushing his opposition."

"How do you know all that?"

I shrug. "I like Greek and Roman history."

Ari rolls his eyes at me.

"Her Greek counterpart is Gaia. Let me do a quick search and see what comes up." I type in my phone. "Not much more than that other than the festival held in her honor was on April the fifteenth. Then pages and pages of info of pretty much the same. I'm not seeing it used in any other way."

"Could it be the name of a terrorist organization?"

"Let me see. Hmm. There's an old Spanish terrorist group that seems to have existed from the late seventies until the mid-eighties. They wanted their own state. They finally came to peace with the government and announced their dissolution. There's been nothing about them since."

"What if it has been revived?" Ari asks.

"I don't know. I don't see anything more about it or

anything else."

"Seems like a dead end. Oh, and it seems Peter and Allie are joining us in Montrovia. I'm putting them in separate bedrooms, just so you know."

I laugh. "Uh, oh."

"Speaking of that. Daniel got called back to the Embassy immediately upon news of the attack on the castle, but he did mention he planned to be at the casino tonight. We should be there, too."

PETER AND ALLIE arrive just after sundown. Peter has already booked dinner reservations at the Michelin-starred restaurant we vetoed the other night. Allie gives me air kisses and rushes to her room to freshen up and change for dinner. Their plane was delayed due to weather, and they are running behind schedule. Peter informs us that we mustn't be late for our reservations, so I run up to my room to change into a cocktail dress.

DINNER WORKS IN our favor. Not only do we have an incredible meal, but Peter is joined in the bar afterwards by the Prince's cousins. We meet the eldest of the sisters, Ophelia, as well as her boyfriend, Viktor. Ophelia is slender with a lean yoga body and short, dark hair that frames her petite face. She's smart, sarcastic, and a leader—almost to the point of domineering. She's dressed in a severely cut dark green suit, black pumps, and a large angular black hat. She has mastered the art of resting bitch face and looking bored. Her boyfriend, Viktor, is much more gregarious. He's friendly, has an aristocratic air, impeccable manners, and can throw down quite a lot of alcohol. He seems fine with Ophelia wearing the pants in their relationship of six months. Viktor and Peter are well acquainted, having vacationed together with their families because of their fathers' friendship.

Younger sister, Clarice, looks exactly like Ophelia would with long hair, but that's where the similarities end. Clarice has more of a laid-back, hippie vibe. Her passion is travel, and she entertains us with stories of trips to exotic locales and her focus on charities that attempt to make the world a better place. Her boyfriend, Armend, who I find out she's only been seeing for a few weeks, is quiet but controlling. She's super laid back, and it surprises me when he looks at her and barks out an order—like *My drink is empty*—and she immediately scurries to remedy it. Plus, his predatory gaze gives me the creeps. My gut reaction is not to trust him, and my mind runs through scenarios. The kind of scenarios where he could be in on the plot to overthrow the monarchy. And it gets me wondering if that's even the plan. What if the plan isn't *just* to kill the Prince? What if it includes bossy, outspoken, and uncontrollable Ophelia? Or controlling an easy to manipulate Clarice? I imagine her and Armend married and him running the show.

AFTER QUITE A few drinks at the bar, the group decides to head to The Casino. I'm back at the roulette table and am winning.

The Prince and Daniel show up late. When the Prince catches my eye, I glare at him, causing him to put his head down and retreat, going off to greet Peter.

Daniel doesn't say anything, just takes up a position across the table from me, so I can't help but look into those baby blues. When a woman starts flirting with him, it distracts me. It's hard to pay attention to everyone around me—constantly scan the room for possible threats or clues—and keep playing, all while controlling my urge to rip the woman's arm off Daniel's chest.

Dang, I just lost a thousand euros.

By the time she's bought him a drink and puts her hand in his hair, I'm down another two. I take my remaining chips from the table and bow out. Honestly, I'm ready to go home. All of a sudden, the excitement of today hits me, and I'm exhausted.

Or maybe it's just an excuse to get out of here before I act irrationally and shoot a midnight dart into the woman, who must be nearly forty, to keep her away from Daniel.

Instead, I belly up to the bar.

Daniel leaves the woman, joins me, and orders us each a beer.

It makes me want to kiss him.

"I heard you have a hot car," he says by way of greeting.

"I have a lot of hot things."

"Don't I know it." He sees me looking over at the group surrounding the Prince. "Are you going to forgive him? He feels terrible."

"Ari said the Embassy came and got you. Do you know what happened? Who the men were?"

"Our government is researching their backgrounds. Were you scared?"

"Yes. Very," I reply with what is expected. Honestly, I was more excited than scared.

"The shooters' nationalities were a surprise," he admits.

"How so?"

"One was German and the other Moroccan, but our government expects a terrorist organization will take credit."

"Credit for what? They could have opened fire on the crowd touring the castle. It wasn't terror. It felt like they were coming after the royal family. The Prince, specifically."

"Another theory is that it was a test," Daniel says,

following what Ari and I had theorized. "That something bigger is to come."

"That's scary."

"Don't worry, Huntley. I'll protect you." God, he's sweet. "Uh, oh. Enzo is making a beeline toward us."

I don't have a chance to reply before the Prince says to me, "You are understandably mad, but put yourself in my position."

"Your position? You were freaking out. I got you out of there. If that's how you treat your friends, I don't want to be one of them."

"Please, I'm sorry. They're just trying to keep me safe."

"Which means we should be on the same side, because that's what I tried to do, too. Keep us *both* safe."

"Please allow me to make it up to you," the Prince pleads.

I roll my eyes, causing Daniel to say, "Come on, Huntley. It's no fun when you're mad. Come to the club with us."

"You two have fun. I have other plans. If you'll excuse me, my friends are here."

I walk a few steps away to join the British lads, who recently arrived. Wesley gives me a kiss on the lips in greeting and places his hand on my ass.

From my position, I can also still hear Daniel and the Prince talking. Ari gives me a wink and joins them. He had been discreetly listening to our conversation about the gunmen.

"I don't know what your people did to her today," I hear Ari say to the Prince, piling on the guilt, "but she got home and just started bawling."

Daniel returns to my side, pulling me away from my British love fest. "Ari told us that you cried when you got home."

"It was kind of an emotional day," I state flatly.

"Just go talk to him. Tell him you're sorry. Make up."

"Tell him *I'm* sorry? Are you freaking kidding me, Daniel? Did he not tell you how he panicked? How he was ready to go out into the hall where the gunfire was? Did he tell you they fired shots into the room we were in, and it was only due to my quick thinking that we got out of there?"

"No, he didn't."

"And you didn't care to know. You two have fun at the club."

I turn on my heels and walk away. I'm not sure what I look like on the outside—hopefully poised and self-assured, but I don't feel that way on the inside. I feel like my being mad at Daniel and the Prince is very real. I'm pissed at them both.

And that scares me.

Rule number one is to never get emotionally attached, because that makes you—and them—vulnerable.

I wonder if I'm really cut out for this job. Being the best in the academy doesn't mean anything in the real world. Could I be like the college football player who wins the Heisman but never has a successful professional career?

I go lock myself in a bathroom stall, taking a deep breath and cleansing myself of all negative thoughts.

A vision of my mother getting shot slips to the forefront of my mind.

It does that when I relax.

I had counseling at Blackwood to help me deal with the trauma of losing my parents, if such a thing is possible. My Uncle Sam told me that my parents got involved with some nasty people in their business dealings. He asked me what I wanted to do with my life. I answered simply: I wanted revenge. I wanted to hunt down the man and kill him myself. He confided in me that he had connections with the government and then offered me a place at Blackwood along with the promise of becoming skilled enough to take on my parents' killer.

When I close my eyes again, I picture the assassin's eyes, and I know that my first mission will be a success.

Because it has to be.

For my country.

For my parents.

But, mostly, for myself.

I return to the casino floor and walk straight over to Ari, who is in a group chatting with Daniel and the Prince.

"Don't wait up for me," I say, patting him on the back as I walk by.

Then I make my way over to an incredibly hot Italian guy whose father designs the suits he wears. He was flirting with me at the roulette table earlier and invited me to go dancing with him. I allow him to lead me out of The Casino and into a nearby club. Then I feign a headache and go home.

When I get there, I ask Ellis for intel on both of the Prince's cousins as well as their boyfriends' backgrounds. Then I scan my room for bugs and destroy them. I can't deal with knowing someone is listening to me. They will probably be replaced soon, but for now, I don't want them to hear the doubt in my head.

I'M IN MY bed, trying to sleep, when I hear a noise outside my terrace door. I grab the gun from my bedside table and proceed cautiously, flattening my back against the wall and then peeking out from behind the curtains.

Daniel is standing under the light.

I put the gun away and open the door. "What are you doing?"

"I was afraid you weren't going to be here. You told Ari not to wait up. I figured you went home with that guy."

"I was mad. My pathetic attempt to get back at you and the Prince for being jerks. I'm not going to sleep with some random guy."

"Like the Prince?"

"I haven't slept with the Prince."

"What, he not as sexy as I am?" Daniel says, leaning against the doorjamb and dropping down an overnight bag.

"He's just—I don't know. I thought we were sort of becoming friends. The way they practically accused me of bringing gunmen with me was upsetting."

"You almost sound like you're falling for him."

I don't answer that question. I ask him what I really want to know. "Daniel, why did you come to Montrovia?"

He cups my face in his hands. "I have a good excuse."

"What is it?"

"I was in Paris, spending a few days with my mother before going to Switzerland to shoot a watch commercial with the Swiss bikini team. When the Prince called and asked about you, I figured what the hell. I'd see an old friend. Party for a few days in this beautiful city."

"And the real reason?" I ask softly.

"Because I wanted to see you," he replies, looking sincere. "But I have to leave first thing in the morning."

"That means we have all night," I breathe out, my voice barely above a whisper.

"What's left of it."

"Then you better not waste a second." I step out into the light.

He grins. "You're wearing my shirt."

The next thing I know, our lips collide, and he's throwing me on the bed.

"So you wanted a slumber party?" I tease, kissing him.

He lies on top of me, holding his weight on his arms. "What I want is your hands all over me. Your body all over me. I want you under me. On top of me—"

"And I just want you in me."

"I love how subtle you are," he teases, stripping his shirt off me.

MISSION: DAY FIVE

I WAKE UP to the sound of Daniel packing and getting dressed. He starts to put on a button-down, but grins at me and stops, pulling it back off his arm and sitting on the bed. He pulls the covers down, wraps me in his shirt, and kisses my forehead.

"My shirts look better on you than they do on me. I'll miss you," he says gently.

"Have fun hanging out with the bikini team."

"That *was* the plan."

"And now?"

"I'm not sure," he says softly as he kisses me. "I'll be back for the race and the big ball. Don't become a princess while I'm gone."

I scoff at him.

"I don't think you'd make a good princess, anyway,"

he says.

"Why's that?"

"I can't imagine he's as good in bed as I am."

"Just because I slept with you—thinking I'd never see you again—doesn't mean that I sleep around. I don't go home with a different man every night."

"But you have quite a bit of previous experience?"

"None of your business."

"Do you want to know mine?"

"No, it's been splashed all over the tabloids that my friend used to obsess over."

"She obsessed over me? Maybe I should meet her."

"She obsessed over the tabloids, Daniel."

"Good. I'd rather have you obsess over me. You have to admit it was good."

"The pizza *was* by far the best I've ever had."

He pushes me against the headboard and gives me a smoking hot kiss.

"I'm not looking to get serious with anyone, Daniel. My life is—"

"Shh. Don't ruin our night with excuses. Go back to sleep."

"IT SEEMS YOU have an admirer," Ari says, waking me up around noon with a very large bouquet of pink roses.

My heart does a little flip thinking they could be from Daniel.

I rub my eyes as Ari sets them on my desk and plucks an envelope out of the arrangement. He's followed into the room by our housekeeper who places a large gift-wrapped box on my bed and then retreats. On top of it is a formal invitation with my name in a gorgeous gold calligraphy.

Ari plops down on the bed as I brush my hair off my face and fluff it. I'm sure it's a freaking mess.

He narrows his eyes, surveying me and then my messy bed. "If I didn't know you were home early and alone last night, I'd think you had a night filled with sex."

"I had a restless sleep," I say, attempting to explain the rumpled sheets and the duvet strewn across the floor.

"You always sleep in a man's shirt?"

I arch an eyebrow at my fake brother. "Sometimes I just sleep naked."

He rolls his eyes and picks up the phone on my bed-side table. "My sister and I would like to have brunch on her terrace."

"Could you ask the chef to make me something hearty? Maybe a grilled cheese and roasted tomato sandwich?"

I'm starved. Must be from all the calories I burned with Daniel last night.

Ari lets the kitchen know what we'd like and then holds up the invitation. "This is from the Queen."

"So, the flowers must be from the Prince," I say, hiding my personal disappointment even though I am actually professionally thrilled they're from him. It means he's interested. I pop the seal, pull the card out, and read aloud. "*Please accept these flowers as a token of my sincerest apologies regarding the events yesterday. I would be delighted to have you accompany me to the Queen's Garden Party today as well as the fashion show this evening. Sincerely, Lorenzo.*" I open the larger gilded envelope to find an inner envelope with both my name and Ari's, followed by a formal invitation to the party. I toss it to him. "Looks like you're invited, too."

"You're playing him well," Ari says. "I'm impressed. I'm also impressed with your quick thinking yesterday. I wasn't sure if you were just theory and promise."

"Isn't this your first mission, too?"

"Yes."

"Do you think you could kill someone if you had to?" I ask, tilting my head. Sometimes I wonder if I could really do it. Hitting targets with rubber bullets and in simulations is a lot different than seeing it happen in front of you. I should know.

"Absolutely," he says, straightening up. "I'm confident in my abilities."

"So we're both well-trained and prepared, but neither of us is field tested. Ari, what was your mission? Like, what did they tell you?"

"No one told me anything, really. I received an envelope. Inside it was a single card with my mission. To uncover the person or persons behind the plot to assassinate the Prince of Montrovia."

"What color was it? The envelope."

"It was pink and covered with glitter, rainbows, and unicorns." He rolls his eyes at me. "What do you think? It was a nondescript white envelope with a white card inside with black ink." He studies me. "What color was yours?"

"Same," I lie, realizing that my mission was slightly different. While I, too, was ordered to uncover the plot, my mission varied in that I am supposed to also both protect the Prince and eliminate those responsible. I think about my training. I was taught to kill a man with nothing more than a paper clip. I can tail a mark without his knowledge. And, once during training, I jumped out of a three-story building using an embroidered hankie as a parachute. I was the star student at Blackwood Academy. Only instead of excelling at normal school extracurricular activities, I'm an expert marksman, unbeaten in hand-to-hand combat, and impossible for even the school's best to tail. "Is that all it said?"

"Isn't that enough?"

"Yeah, it is," I lie, opening the gift. Inside are three smaller boxes. One with the golden gown I was trying on the day I met the Prince.

"That's quite the dress," Ari says, as I hold up the dreamy golden masterpiece. Under the gown are a pair of Jimmy Choo sandals and a complementary clutch.

"I had it on when we met. Well, actually, I was looking at ties when we met, but then he came over to the women's side and introduced himself when I was standing in front of the mirror in this.

"Must have made an impression. Do you think this will work? Getting close to him? I feel like being close to him might only allow us to protect him. To react to an attempt."

"My orders were a little different than yours," I confess.

"How were they different?"

"I was told to get close to and protect him." I don't mention the part about killing the bad guys.

"So I'm the sleuth, and you're the bodyguard?"

I shrug. "Maybe. But I think you're right. We have to figure out who's behind this. I feel like we aren't making any progress."

"I wish we could have interrogated the gunmen," Ari says. "Maybe we could have gotten some clues."

"The fact that a group hasn't claimed them by now leads me to believe we can rule out the major terrorist groups." I open the other box to find a demure pink crepe dress with an Alexander McQueen label.

"Terrorist organizations are infiltrating all areas of

the world. It could be a smaller group," Ari counters. "What's in the last box?"

"Oh! It's a hat!" I place it on my head and stand in front of the mirror over my desk. "Look at the beautiful sweeping brim. And the roses and feathers are so pretty!"

"You're going to look like royalty in that," he teases. "I think the Prince fancies you."

I roll my eyes. "He probably sends invites and dresses to lots of girls."

He holds up a card. "Did you not see the note in the hat box?"

"No. What does it say?"

"*I'm honored to custom design your millinery for the Queen's Garden Party. Best, Anna Remaldi.*" Ari sets the hat down and pulls out his phone, clicking buttons. "It says here that Anna is the Royal milliner for the Queen of Montrovia."

"Wow. Okay, maybe he does fancy me a bit. But that's the goal, right?"

"Yes, it is. So at the Garden Party, let's try to spend more time with the cousins. We need to figure out if they are threats or targets."

"And I want to find out more about the gunmen. Who they were. Who they were working for."

"You think they're mercenaries not terrorists?"

"I think we have to consider that possibility. What if there is something bigger at play here? Most terror happens in protest. Some is simply to disrupt the governments they are against. The biggest terror group now says their ultimate goal is to overthrow governments of unstable, heavily Muslim nations and establish their own state." I pause. "Which doesn't really fit Montrovia. I read that about ninety percent of the country is Roman Catholic."

"But it's a jewel of great wealth."

"So where does the *Terra* thing fit in?" I wonder.

"I think terra sounds a lot like terror."

Our server taps on the door and enters with a tray of food.

"Looks like it's time to eat," Ari says. "I expect Allie will be up to join you soon. An invitation to the party was delivered for her and Peter as well."

A SHORT TIME later, Allie is at my door.

"You awake?" she whispers.

"We're out on the terrace. Come join us."

She's still wrapped in a robe and looks like she just woke up.

"Did you get an invitation to the Queen's Garden Party?" she asks.

"We did."

"What are you going to wear?"

"The Prince sent me an outfit and a hat."

"I looked online to see what Kate Middleton wears

when she goes to these sorts of things in Britain. Usually a proper suit or a tailored dress and always a hat. I have a floral dress that will work, but no hat. Do you think they wear them here?"

"Yes, they do. What color is your dress? I have a hat you could borrow. Or we could send the boys out to shop."

Ari groans. "I think since I'm finished with breakfast, I'll leave the fashion to you ladies and go have a pint with Peter."

"Oh, he'd love that," Allie says. "I'll get my dress and be right back."

I finish my meal and take a deep breath. I had hoped to do some yoga and work out, but now I'm going to have to hustle to be ready in time. I'm pretty sure you shouldn't show up fashionably late to the Queen's party.

I consider sending her son a text thanking him for the gifts, but decide it's better for the mission to keep him wondering if I'll show up.

"Here's my dress," Allie says, returning. "What do you think?" She's holding it up to herself. "Too short?"

"It almost comes to your knee. I think it will work. And the black background with the floral pattern is both modern and traditional." I have no idea what that even meant. My fashion decisions usually revolve around which black yoga pants make my butt look the best. She nods like I made sense.

"Oh, good. Ellis told me you have hair and makeup on call. Have you called them?"

I go into my closet and grab a hatbox. The Kates sent me with two hats. One to wear to a daytime party and one to wear to the beach. "No, but I'm sure Ellis did. He's on top of things."

Ellis knocks on the door just as I'm pulling the hat out of the box.

"Hair and makeup will arrive in one hour. We are on a tight time frame, and you don't want to be late."

"We won't be. Allie, what do you think? Shall we pre-party with some champagne?"

"Most definitely."

"I will send a server back shortly. Miss Allie, would you like something to eat?"

"Oh, yes. A spinach salad, no dressing. Maybe some grilled salmon or chicken on it?" She turns to me. "I told my agent I was coming here, and she booked me in the fashion show tonight at the Amber Room. Can you come? Will you bring Daniel?"

"Daniel went to Switzerland. Something to do with a photo shoot."

"Have you seen that ad he's in? The one where he is swimming with the waterproof watch on?" She picks up my extra hat and fans her face with it. Then she realizes what she's doing and looks at the hat. "Oh, this is adorable. And the black will match my dress. Are you sure I can borrow it?"

"I'm sure."

"So do you like the Prince or Daniel? You had a lot of chemistry at the gala. And the way you danced together—it was almost magical."

"Magical?" I scoff. "Uh, no. It was just a few dances."

"And then you left together."

"We got pizza."

"I got some pizza of my own. Do you know about me and Ari? Do you think badly of me?"

"I think all that matters is what you think of yourself. I personally have no problem with you sleeping with whomever you fancy. Unless you have some kind of a commitment with Peter."

"Oh, no. He's told me *many times* he doesn't *do* commitment. I know he goes through women, but he's really sweet, and I do enjoy his company. It's just that he's not—how can I put this delicately? Your brother is a beast in the sack. And I feel like an addict waiting for my next hit. Staying at your villa is both brilliant and torturous. I snuck into his room last night."

"I try to stay out of his love life."

"You just found out he's your brother. Admit it. The first time you saw him he heated up your panties."

"I did think he was nice looking."

"You two look a lot alike. I looked up your dad online. He must have had dominant genes, because you both look just like him."

I make a mental note to find a photo of Ares and have a look myself, but am now even more impressed with our casting. I'm lost in thought and not really paying attention to the fact that Allie is rummaging through my handbag. She pulls something out of it.

"Oh, I should borrow one of these. Flights seem to clog my pores." She starts to take the back off one of the strips.

"Wait!" I yell, ripping it out of her hands, imagining her beautiful nose blown off by the incendiary device.

She's taken aback by my outburst.

"Sorry," I reply. "It's just I need to throw those away. They're cheap and practically ripped half the skin off my nose. It was red for two days. You wouldn't want that for the fashion show tonight."

She clutches her chest as if I just saved her life. "Oh, thank goodness you stopped me. I would have been so upset if that happened!"

"Me too," I say, taking all the strips out of my bag and throwing them in the trash. I'll retrieve them when she goes to get changed.

GETTING INTO THE Queen's Garden Party is much different than driving to the castle with the Prince. Vehicles are not parked onsite, but rather valeted. All guests must show their invitation and identification then pass through a metal detector and have their bags checked. My shoes go off even though they aren't outfitted with any gadgets, since they were a gift from the Prince. The shoes aren't X-rayed as they should be, simply run past the nose of a bomb-sniffing dog that gives them a cursory whiff. There are a fair number of armed military present, both watching the crowd and surrounding the castle.

I'm relieved to see it. It wouldn't deter a well-trained assassin, but it is a good defense against suicide bombers or armed attacks.

Allie and Peter are held up in security, so Ari escorts me toward the garden, and we talk while winding down the brick, tree-lined path. Flowers are in full bloom, and the hedges expertly tended.

"Let's go over the weak spots in security," he says, speaking low so that no one will overhear us. "There are snipers on the roof. The castle is surrounded by soldiers with assault weapons. They brought in portable restrooms so that visitors will have no reason to enter the castle. The guests have been personally invited and, I'm sure, pre-screened. What would you do if you wanted to kill the Prince today?"

I look at the brick walls surrounding the garden then up at the sky. "Maybe fly in?"

"A helicopter would be susceptible to the snipers."

"It could do a lot of damage before it was taken out,

though. What about an armed drone? They are quiet and could sneak up. But, honestly, I'd be more worried about the backend of the event. The food delivery trucks, the caterers, the servers. Or, worse, someone like us."

"What do you mean?" Ari asks.

"We got through. Do you have any weapons in your possession?"

"No, the invitation mentioned security, so I'm not packing."

I grab his wrist. "What about your watch?"

"Cartier, brand new."

I show him mine. "My Cartier is special."

"How so?"

"It's loaded with poison darts." I flash my hand at him. "And this ring can reveal a single-use poison tip. If I scratched you with it, you'd be dead in a matter of minutes. If I were playing for the other side, *I'd* be the big threat. And I'd succeed easily."

"My sister is a badass," he says, and it makes me smile. It's the first mission-related compliment he's given me.

"Don't you have any gadgets?"

"Yeah, I do." He rolls his eyes like a little boy caught with candy.

"What do you have?"

"A fine writing pen that when clicked properly contains a similar dart. Cuff links that become tracking and listening devices. A hankie square made of Kevlar."

"My brother is a badass," I tease.

"So that's what we need to be looking for—someone like us. But I agree with you. The threat could be a man or woman and could be either a guest or server. Keep your eyes open and stick by the Prince. I'll stay close by, as well, forming a sort of outer perimeter."

"Sounds like a plan," I agree as we arrive at the entrance to the garden.

"Wait up!" Allie calls from behind us, her and Peter scurrying to catch up.

"That was ridiculous," Peter huffs. "To be invited to an event and have to practically be strip searched."

"What happened?"

"He had a nail file in his pocket," Allie states.

Peter goes on. "Clearly, it is not a weapon. What could I even do with it? File their royal nails until they bled?"

Ari and I share a glance, both thinking the same thing. There are a lot of things you can do with a nail file, jabbing it directly into a man's eye being the first that comes to mind.

"Why do you have a nail file? They don't allow them on airplanes," Ari states.

"I don't think Peter's ever flown commercial." Allie smiles.

"And it wasn't big," Peter continues. "Just a pair of

clippers. I'm prone to hangnails."

Clippers can be effective, too, I think. With the right amount of force and a quick slash, a major artery in the neck could be opened and a man would bleed to death. Messy, but effective.

"They didn't let me keep them. That's what took so long. I had to fill out a coat check type form. If they weren't made of gold and a gift from my grandfather, I would have just ditched them." He grabs Allie's hand. "Remind me to pick them up when we leave."

"I'm sure after the attack on the castle yesterday, they aren't taking any chances, for all our sakes," Ari says.

"Still, pain in my arse," Peter replies.

WE GO THROUGH an arched trellis to enter the large, perfectly manicured, green-lawned garden. It's beautiful. Stately trees surround its perimeter. A mammoth ornate marble fountain punctuates its center. Smaller floral trees line the center paths and numerous iron benches allow for gazing at the floral displays. We are quickly greeted by a white-gloved server offering us champagne from a silver tray.

We each take a glass and Peter says, "Here's to new friends and fast cars. Thanks for talking us into coming here."

We clink our glasses and I take a sip, the bubbles tickling my nose.

"Looks like there's food over there," Ari says. If Ari has one mission weakness, it's his need to constantly eat. He must still be growing.

We're halfway to the buffet when I see the Prince making a beeline toward us. He greets everyone, then pulls me away from the group.

"You look stunning. I wasn't sure if you received the delivery." He looks at the ground, fidgets a bit, then looks at me with sincerity written all over his face. "I didn't know if you would come. Does this mean you forgive me?"

"That depends. Do you think I had anything to do with the men at the castle yesterday?"

He takes my hand. "No, I do not. It's just that I surprised them with our visit." He looks around and lowers his voice. "You can't be in a leadership role in any country in today's world and not be threatened. That is the downside to dating me."

"Is this a date?"

He touches my face tenderly. "I certainly would like it to be."

"Then I accept your apology."

He smiles then seals it with a sweet kiss. "And you mustn't leave my side all day. It will likely be a stuffy affair but is filled with interesting and prominent people from around the world. Many of whom you will be seeing more of during the weekend's festivities."

I turn and scan the crowd. "I'd like to meet them all, then," I say, hoping it will help me uncover the plot and find the bad guys.

His eyes brighten. "Really?"

"Of course."

"Let's start by greeting my mother, the host of this event. You should know it was only with her help that I was able to attain the hat."

"The hat is my favorite thing. The only kind of hat I've ever worn is a baseball cap. And a beret once when I tried to dress French."

The Prince laughs. "You are adorable." His hand moves to the small of my back as he escorts me across the lawn. He's moving at a good clip, his fast pace probably signaling that he doesn't want to stop to chat along the way.

The Queen greets me with an actual hug— something Europeans don't usually do to acquaintances. "Thank you for helping my son stay out of danger yesterday," she whispers.

"You're welcome."

"There's someone I'd like you to meet." She gestures to a woman standing on her left. "Anna, I'd like to present to you Huntley Von Allister. Your work looks stunning on her." She points to my hat, or fascinator, whichever this technically is.

"It's a pleasure to meet you, Miss Von Allister.

Would you mind taking a picture with me?"

I say sure and then the Queen decides to join us. The milliner's arms aren't very long, so I use her phone to take a selfie of the three of us.

Then I'm introduced to a whole lot of people. So many that even with my excellent memory for details, it's hard to keep track. I was hoping someone would stand out. Look nervous, smarmy, or like a killer, but they don't.

ONCE WE'VE MADE the rounds, we work our way back to where we started, with Peter, Allie, and Ari who are chatting with the Prince's cousins and their boyfriends.

The Prince excuses himself, telling me he'll be right back.

My initial assessment of Clarice's boyfriend, Armend, is correct. His eyes affect me in a negative way. I should be keeping watch on him, just in case. The fact that they met only a few weeks ago and he's suddenly here in the midst of royalty is bothersome.

Of course, I suppose the same could be said of me. I've known the Prince for all of three days. But it's Ophelia's boyfriend who I can't stop watching. Viktor looks very uncomfortable. Nervous. He's sweating and fidgety. I run what little about him I know through my head. Family chum of Peter Prescott. Father originally from Russia, who owns an international shipping business and as a hobby became the top yacht builder in the world. Mother is a well-known retired French prima ballerina whose father held a senior minister position in the French government.

Viktor has one hand in his pocket and is looking more and more nervous.

Like someone about to commit a crime, possibly?

Clarice turns to Peter. "Just yesterday I was telling my friend who joined the Peace Corps about your father's new interests in the world's water. I don't believe anyone should be allowed to own our water. It should be free to all. But he's been buying up water around the world. I'd like to talk to him about the Terra Project."

I quell any reaction I have when I hear those words. Ari and I share a glance.

"What's the Terra Project?" he asks.

"It's a resource based economy, where all people will share and work together to build a better future world. Everyone would have equal access to shelter, water, healthcare, and food. It's about changing incentives and technological processes on a global scale. For example, there would be no monetary system."

"It seems hard to imagine a world without money," Peter says haughtily. "Can't see my dad being interested in that."

"Well, a long time ago, before there was money and power, people bartered for everything. The idea is also to take care of our planet by becoming a green society."

I'm trying to focus on what she's saying, but I can't because Viktor still has one hand in his pocket and is looking more and more nervous. He takes out his hankie and wipes sweat from his brow.

"Hot one today," he states to no one in particular.

"Why don't you take off your jacket?" I suggest.

"Uh, no," he says, and I'm really starting to worry about what's in his pocket.

Or under his jacket.

When the Prince strides toward us, Viktor starts to move.

I'm on edge, ready to pounce on him at the first sign of a weapon. If we were closer to the trees, I'd pull him out of sight and search him, but that's not possible.

The Prince winks at me and takes my hand. Then he asks all of us, including Viktor—who now looks as if he's about to have a stroke—to join him at the fountain.

We all move in that direction, and I make sure to put myself in position between the Prince and Viktor.

"If everyone could gather around," the Prince announces to the crowd. I glance at the snipers on the roof, to see if they are still paying attention. But if Viktor pulls a gun, the snipers couldn't react quickly enough. It would be up to Ari and me. Ari imperceptibly touches my hand. I know he's thinking what I'm thinking as he moves to flank the other side of the Prince.

The Prince's personal bodyguard apparently is supposed to follow five steps behind because that's exactly where he has been all day. Close, but not close enough, in my opinion.

The crowd does as they are asked and gathers around the fountain.

Viktor looks crazy. Surely, he wouldn't shoot the Prince right here in front of everyone, would he?

Viktor takes Ophelia's hand and gets down on one knee.

"Ophelia Louise Marchesa Vallenta, will you marry me?"

Ophelia doesn't look the least bit surprised by his proposal. She doesn't cry. Doesn't jump up and down. Doesn't jump into his arms and scream.

"I will," she says flatly, like she's closed a business deal not accepted his promise of everlasting love.

They hug and everyone claps.

Viktor's hand finally leaves his pocket, producing a box with a large engagement ring.

I let out a sigh. No wonder he was so damn nervous. Proposing in front of all of these people combined with the fear of losing the ring would make anyone sweat.

Champagne is quickly passed around and the whole group, nearly six hundred in attendance, toast to the happy couple.

"You can thank me for the vintage champagne," the

Prince says, turning to me and clinking my glass.

"Is that where you were off to?"

He smiles at me, takes a sip, and says, "I missed you while I was gone."

"You were gone for a very short while."

"I expected to come back and find you surrounded by men."

"There are snipers on the roof of your castle. Somehow I doubt anyone would choose today to try to steal your date."

He laughs. It's an easy, sexy laugh followed by another sweet kiss, which causes me to relax.

WE'RE STILL IN the crowd around the newly engaged when Clarice asks me about yesterday's attack. "I heard you were here."

"Lorenzo wanted to give me a tour."

"Of the royal bed chamber, no doubt," someone mumbles.

"Although, first I met his father," I continue, ignoring the snide comment. The people around us were all chattering up a storm, but when I mention visiting the King, a hush spreads over the area as all eyes turn toward me.

"You met King Vallenta?" Clarice asks. "That's a big deal."

"Why?"

"Because Enzo never introduces the women he dates to his parents," she explains.

Lorenzo squeezes my hand, clearly uncomfortable with where this conversation is going.

"Well, maybe that's why he did. We aren't dating," I reply with a shrug.

"No, you don't understand. He wouldn't introduce his father to anyone he wasn't serious about romantically. Isn't that right, Enzo?"

The Prince doesn't reply, instead he pulls me away from the group.

"Please, don't listen to them. Everyone is on my case about taking a wife."

"It's okay. I can handle it."

"At least Ophelia is older than me, so she should be getting married before I do."

"Do you like Viktor?"

"Of course, he and I go way back. He can be a bit of a cad, but he's certainly well-connected. I'm convinced that he and Peter Prescott will eventually own the world someday. So, we would do well to be friends with them."

"What makes you say that?" I ask seriously.

"I'm joking," he laughs. "I just meant that eventually they will take over for their fathers, just as I will. Although Peter says he wants to cash out and enjoy life, Viktor is more driven. He's already training to transition into a leadership role within his father's conglomerate over the next few years." He stops talking and looks around for a moment. "Sometimes I wish I could do that."

"Cash out and enjoy life?"

"Yes, what do you think of my life so far?"

"I'm not sure what I think of your life, but you, personally, surprise me."

"How so?"

"Everything I've read had you in a different woman's bed every night. I guess I just haven't seen that."

"You can't believe everything you read."

"Are you saying that you haven't slept with a lot of women?"

He purses his lips, suddenly realizing this conversation, for a man, is like walking through a minefield. "I haven't slept with anyone since I met you."

I laugh. "Three whole days, huh?"

"Spending time with me can be difficult. Earlier you took a photo with the hat maker." He holds up his phone and shows me the photo on the woman's social media account along with her post: *A hat designed especially for this lovely girl at the request of HRH Queen Vallenta. Could we be looking at our future Princess?*

"This will kick-start things," he explains. "Combined with the fact I was serious when I said I'd like you to escort me to all the events this week. For the race there is much media, and you will be photographed with me at every turn. And now that they know I introduced you to my parents, along with what's about to happen next—"

"What's about to happen next?" I should know the answer to this. I should be constantly aware of my surroundings—but my gaze has been held by the Prince, his sincerity and honesty evident.

He turns me around so that I can see his father, the King, walking straight toward us and flanked on his sides and rear by the Royal Guard. It's quite the processional. Once he arrives, he greets me with a warm embrace, like we're old friends.

"Any chance I could get a ride in that car?" he asks me.

"I might even let you drive."

"Today, after all these people leave, maybe? Then you can join us for dinner."

"I'd like that."

The King greets his son and then moves to the other side of the fountain to be with his wife.

People around us are now murmuring about me.

This is crazy. I was taught to blend in. To live life under the radar. Being this exposed makes me feel like I'm caught in the crosshairs.

This is a very odd mission. I was trained for six years to be the best and, now, I'll probably never be able to fly under the radar again. Which seems counterproductive. If Ari's right and this is our permanent cover, it doesn't make sense. If we succeed in our mission and uncover the plot and kill the bad guys, then what? What's next?

Regardless of what Ari says about us being undercover in plain sight, I get a sinking sensation in my gut, knowing that succeeding at this mission may just make my career as a field agent very short.

AFTER THE PARTY dies down, the Prince leads me to his residence. "Thank you for agreeing to stay for dinner. It means a lot to me."

"You're welcome. Am I dressed okay?"

"You are. Dinner with just my parents will be a casual affair."

"That's good. So, were you worried about having all these people here after what happened yesterday?"

"Not in the least. I trust our police and army. We are a small country with very little petty crime. Our citizens are well off. Tourism brings a flood of money, and we cater to the wealthy of the world."

"But with wealth does there not come crime? Russian billionaires, arms dealers, drug kingpins, organized crime?"

"Of course, but when they come to Montrovia, they come to celebrate their spoils, not to work. Maybe that is the difference. Our country demands refinement. We have the best of the best. Did you know that every hotel in Montrovia is five star?" he asks, leading me to his bedroom. I take off my shoes and hat, and we relax on the bed.

"I think I read that somewhere."

He quickly changes the subject. "Would you let me drive your car before my father gets to?"

"Hmm, not a chance," I say, pulling him to my lips.

We kiss. Sweetly. Softly. It's nice.

And intimate in an unusual way. I find myself enjoying it very much. It's been awhile since I've done nothing but make-out with a guy. Usually kissing is just a prelude to sex. This is more like a prelude to something else.

Especially when I fall asleep in his arms.

WE'RE WOKEN LATER in the evening and told that dinner with his parents has been cancelled. His father was exhausted from his appearance today and is resting.

The Prince gets dressed for the evening's festivities and then I let him drive. I had texted Ellis earlier and had him drop off the car.

"Your car is a quite the tease," he says, rolling slowly through town.

"She prefers to go fast, for sure," I agree, constantly looking in the side mirror to be sure the black car holding his bodyguards—of which there are four tonight—is still behind us. "What time does the fashion show start?"

He checks his watch. "The party started about an

hour ago, but the fashion show won't start until later."

"I don't want to miss Allie walking the runway. She's really excited about it."

"Why is that?"

"She's popular in the United States, but hasn't done much internationally."

"She is a very attractive woman. I'm sure she will do splendidly and have many admirers after tonight. My eyes, however, will only be on you."

"That will be awkward," I tease, leading him into my suite after arriving at the villa and asking for a bottle of champagne to be sent up.

THE PRINCE IS poking around my bathroom while I touch up my makeup. He holds up a round blue object. "Why do you have so many blue balls?"

I stop brushing my hair to see what he's talking about.

"They're bath bombs."

"Sounds quite dangerous. It's interesting what you brought with you."

It *is* interesting what the Kates outfitted the villa with. I'm pretty sure one of them is obsessed with Lush products and imagined me in a foreign country without the ability to take a proper bath. She even included a note on her favorite combinations, thankfully.

"Honestly, I didn't bring that much. I read that

Montrovian shops have everything your heart could possibly desire. I just wasn't sure if they had these, so I shopped in bulk." I walk over to a large glass container and pull out a gold bar. "This gold one is perfect before a night out, because it gives your skin a soft shimmer. But my favorite thing is to mix a blue one with the gold. The combination looks like you're bathing with a mermaid."

"I'd like to bathe with a mermaid."

"Since you've slept with all the other girls in the world, you need to find a new species?" I laugh. I'm funny sometimes.

"I'd like to take one with you."

"My bath tub is built for one, and there's a reason for that."

"Why?"

"Baths are a solitary activity. A way to relax."

"Have you never taken a bath with a friend?"

"No, I haven't."

"We must remedy that immediately. The art of bathing can be very sensual."

"Let me guess, you were bathed by nannies even after you hit puberty."

He shrugs. "I was raised to—I'm comfortable naked."

"I'm not."

"I've seen you in a bikini. You looked plenty comfortable."

"My lady bits were hidden."

"In Montrovia, topless sunbathing is encouraged."

"I don't have a problem with that."

"Then tomorrow, we have a date. You will bring the bath bombs. I will supply the bathing garments."

THE AMBER ROOM is a glittering venue set up specifically for the Montrovian Grand Prix and is the setting for numerous parties over the race weekend. There is flowing champagne, exquisite cuisine, performances by iconic artists, amped up DJ sets, and tonight's fashion show which benefits an international charity. I've met jet-setters, film stars, Formula One drivers, and royalty from numerous nations. Security is tight, and no one gets in unless they are on the list.

I'm having fun.

And feeling fairly relaxed. With all the famous people in the room, the bodyguards and security are numerous. Not to mention that the Prince's personal bodyguard, Juan, is sticking very close tonight as are the other three who accompanied us to this event.

I even get the chance to go backstage to wish Allie luck. I thought she might be nervous, but she seems in her element and ready to go. She also looks killer with her bangs teased and held back by a barrette and wearing a sexy, retro bikini.

I go back out and take a prime seat next to the Prince

as the show starts.

A well-known DJ is spinning a sick beat, and the fashion show is fast-paced, featuring both men and women's attire from many of the high-end boutiques in Cap's elite shopping district.

"You would look amazing in that," Lorenzo says, commenting on the red gown that is the grand finale to the show. "You must have it."

"Where would I wear it? Cinderella's castle?"

"I was thinking my castle," he says, taking my hand in his and kissing it. "Shall I buy you glass slippers, too?"

"I don't know. Do you want me to leave you at midnight?"

He slides his hand into my hair and kisses me. "Most definitely not. Does that mean you will still allow me to escort you to the Queen's Ball?"

"When is it, again?" I ask, playing it cool.

"Sunday night, after the race. It's our grand finale."

"I guess since I said I'd hang out with you for Race Week, it would include that."

"*Hang out* seems so casual."

"I thought that's how you liked your relationships with women."

"Usually, that is the case. With you, I'm inclined not to want such a casual arrangement."

"We've only known each other for a short time."

"Still." He gazes into my eyes. It's incredibly sweet. I

feel a pang of guilt for manipulating his emotions, but I know the manipulation isn't a lie. Because I genuinely like this man.

And I'll be damned if I'm going to let anyone kill him.

There's a psychological phenomenon known as Stockholm Syndrome, where a hostage develops a strong emotional bond, almost a love, for their captor. These feelings are irrational in light of the danger endured by the victim. If the captor is kind to them, they mistake the lack of abuse for caring. It's a form of traumatic bonding. Traumatic bonding can occur in numerous situations, like a hostage and his captor or even in a situation like the Prince and I have been in. Two people in danger together. It heightens the feelings and emotions and is completely natural.

Or so it was explained to us in school. What a good spy has to do, however, is use this closeness to his advantage.

I was taught to be emotionless and uncaring, but no matter how much they tried to drill that into my head, it never worked. I am motivated because of emotion. And it's that emotion that will always drive me to succeed.

THE PRINCE STEPS away to speak to someone in private. This worries me, but I see a Saudi Prince with numerous bodyguards join him.

When he is finished and meets back up with me, he's agitated.

"What's wrong?"

"The Saudis use the Strait of Montrovia to ship oil to the rest of Europe and the U.S. He offered to have his naval assets supplement ours. He is worried that we are vulnerable."

"Are you?"

"Every country is vulnerable to an attack. An elite air force could destroy us, but terror organizations do not command those sorts of troops. When he left the meeting, things were tense. I mean, what did he expect? For me to turn our royal maritime unit over to him?"

"I don't know. Did he say why this is a concern all of a sudden?"

"If you are going to spend time with me, you must know the risks. My national intelligence has intercepted chatter, an indication that something could happen in my country. I'm assuming his government has heard it as well."

"Like a terrorist attack? During the race?"

"It seems to be more indicative of a threat to the throne—to me, personally."

"Considering someone may have just tried to gun you down, that makes sense."

He grins at me and takes my hand. "But you kept me safe. I'll have to be keeping you close."

WE MINGLE FOR a bit longer then end up in a corner of the Amber Room chatting with a wealthy Indian man, who owns one of the race teams, along with his drivers. He's hosting a party on his yacht tomorrow night and assures us that we will receive hand-delivered invitations in the morning. We're all sipping champagne—except for Lorenzo, who guzzled down his last drink, his conversation with the Saudi clearly weighing on his mind.

I'm nodding where appropriate about the upcoming race, but I'm mostly eavesdropping on the conversation behind me. Clarice is discussing the Terra Project with an actress who is a United Nations Goodwill Ambassador. She's sharing her passion for the project and discussing an area in the United States where they've set up a successful trial community using all the Terra concepts. I wonder how this peaceful initiative could be related to a threat to the Prince.

But then she mentions that the next step is to try it somewhere on a larger scale. What if that is her plan? To bring this project to her own country. The country she could be the queen of if just a few people were to die.

That comment alone moves her up to prime suspect number one on my list.

I excuse myself to use the facilities and give Ari a look that lets him know I want to talk in private.

We meet in the hallway to the restrooms.

"Ari, were you listening to Clarice? Did you hear what she said about the Terra Project?"

"I did."

"Do you think that's her plan? To become Queen and implement it for all of Montrovia?"

"I can't imagine that. She seems passionate about a lot of random things."

"That's true. I heard her ranting earlier about the energy used by the cattle industry. She won't eat meat."

"But she sure likes the bone," Ari fires back.

"What?"

"Ha! I don't even know where that came from. Actually, I do. It's from an oldie that one of my instructors used to listen to. Get it?"

"Ari, you have a bone," I say with a smirk. "Maybe you should *barter* her with it."

"She has a boyfriend and seems crazy in love with him. I don't like him though."

"I want to know how she got to be such a tree hugger. How did she learn about this project? Who started the whole idea?"

"I don't know, but we better find out," he says.

LORENZO IS WAITING for me in the corner of the room, chatting now with Peter and Allie.

Clarice still has the actress cornered and is ranting. "Wouldn't it be amazing if our culture didn't thrive on conspicuous consumption? A small nation like ours would be the perfect place to take the project to the next level. That is, if the King would abolish the currency and let us all live in peace."

"It seems pretty peaceful here already," the actress says.

"We do live in peace, but that's not the point. When there were terror attacks in Europe that killed a few hundred people the news was all over it, but when thousands died in genocide in Africa, no one said a word. It's that kind of inequity that the project would change. Not to mention the industries that are ruining our planet. Do you eat meat?"

"Uh, yeah," the actress admits, sounding a bit ashamed.

"Did you know that way back in 2006 a report was released by the Food and Agriculture Organization of the United Nations that states *the livestock sector is a major stressor on many ecosystems and on the planet as a whole*? Did you know that agriculture releases the most greenhouse gas emission, even more than the transportation sector? Not to mention the horrific treatment of the innocent animals."

I think she's going to stop ranting, but she continues. "The industry has even made up names for our food to make us feel better about what we are eating. Instead of Foie gras, escargot, veal, and caviar, we should call them what they are: unnaturally fattened duck livers, snails, baby calves, and fish eggs."

Allie, who must be eavesdropping, too, looks at me and makes a gagging gesture, which causes me to stifle a laugh.

A waiter emerges from a door just behind us with a flute of champagne on a platter and presents it to the Prince. He takes it. I'm thinking it's kind of rude that there's only one glass when I notice that the waiter is wearing black gloves instead of the normal white ones.

A chain reaction quickly takes place in my body. My heart races, my breathing speeds up, and my muscles are on high alert ready to strike.

Something's not right.

In a split second, I process the waiter's military short haircut. Buff body. The tattoo snaking up his neck.

The Prince moves the glass toward his lips.

"Wait! Don't drink that!" I yell, reacting quickly by grabbing his arm.

I give Ari a look and he stealthily leaves the room, hopefully to chase the man, who I watch run out of another door.

Both Lorenzo and I are quickly surrounded by his bodyguards.

Juan, his personal guard, asks me, "Why shouldn't he drink it? What do you know?"

I realize I must act dumb. My being able to stay close

to the Prince depends on them believing what I say next.

"Uh, I don't know anything. I just thought it was weird."

"What was weird?"

"The waiter came out of the kitchen with only one glass of champagne instead of a tray full, and he had on black gloves instead of white ones." I look straight at the Prince. "I mean, I don't know how things go here in Montrovia, but I'd hate to see you end up as a plaything in a frat house getting taken advantage of." I purposefully giggle. "Oh, wait. That doesn't make sense. Maybe I've had too much champagne." What I'm about to say next is a total conflict, but I have to say it. I ready my hand to knock the drink away in case they call my bluff. I'll blow the mission if I have to, to keep him safe. "You're right, I'm being dumb. Who'd bother to roofie the future King? Everyone already knows he's easy. I just reacted, it's probably fine to drink."

The Prince chuckles and considers this by looking at his glass.

"Don't," his bodyguard says sternly. "Give me the glass." He speaks into his cuff, alerting the police, then takes the glass carefully. "Miss Von Allister had a good gut reaction. Better safe than sorry. We'll take care of this. You two enjoy the rest of the party."

ARI TAKES OFF on a run after the black-gloved waiter,

but the man has a large lead.

By the time he gets outside, the man has taken off his waiter's jacket and is hopping onto a motorcycle. Ari presses a button on his phone and communicates with Ellis.

Ellis is moving the limo toward the street when the motorcycle screams its way around the corner. The man is riding a black Ducati with no identification tags. Ellis throws the car into park, jumps out, and taps his cane hard on the ground causing a steel baton to emerge from its core. He sticks the baton out just as the assailant drives by and knocks the man off the bike.

The assailant rolls to the ground with a grunt, but quickly pops up, pulling a slim gun out of his coat and aiming it at Ellis.

Ellis leaps toward him with surprising grace for someone of his age and clips the man with the baton, knocking the gun free. Ari who has been sprinting to catch up, grabs the gun off the pavement and levels it at the man, telling him not to move.

The man doesn't listen. He kicks the gun out of Ari's hand and punches at his face. Ari avoids the contact and throws a series of punches of his own, all connecting and leaving the man dazed. Ari gives the man another blow, knocking him down to the ground.

"Who do you work for?" Ari questions, sitting on top of the man, his hands wrapped around the man's neck, almost cutting off his oxygen.

The man gives Ari a defiant look, then head butts him, causing Ari to go crashing backwards. The man gets up, only to be shot in the arm by Ellis. The man grabs his bicep and attempts to run back to his bike. Ari stops him with another blow to the head just as the authorities arrive. They quickly take the man into custody, thank Ari and Ellis for their service to Montrovia, and leave.

What they don't know is that before they left, Ari managed to place a small tracking and recording device on the man.

Ari and Ellis calmly go back to the limo and follow the police to the detention center.

They record and listen to the authorities' first—and very useless—round of questioning. The assailant refuses to answer anything.

When they take a break, Ari slips unnoticed into the center and into the questioning room, only to find the man dead.

Foam leaks out of his mouth.

Ari takes a vial from his jacket pocket, scoops up some of the foam, and leaves the facility as stealthily as he came.

THE PRINCE LEADS me to the bar where he orders himself a stiff drink. After his earlier uneasy conversation combined with a possible attempted poisoning, I can see why he would need one.

"Would you like to go home now?" I ask him. "It's been a long day."

He gently brushes my hair from my face and kisses me, avoiding telling me what's troubling him and saying instead, "I've enjoyed your company immensely."

"As I have yours."

"I'm looking forward to our bath tomorrow."

"Me too."

He glances at his watch. "I guess it already is tomorrow. How would you feel about coming home with me now?"

I know what he's asking.

I bite the corner of my lip nervously and lower my head slightly. "Um . . ."

He takes his finger and raises my chin. "It's okay. We should move slowly. This. Us."

He leans in to kiss me again, but we are separated by guards. "Come this way, quickly."

We're escorted to a waiting limo and taken to the castle.

I lean toward him and whisper. "Is this really how you get a girl to come home with you?"

He laughs heartily then rolls the partition down and asks Juan what's going on.

"We'll discuss it when we are in the safety of the palace, Your Highness," he replies formally. Usually, he calls him Lorenzo.

When we get there, we're whisked down a hall to the War Room, and I'm introduced to Admiral Philipe Lamonte, the Joint Chief of the Montrovian Armed Forces.

Admiral Lamonte gets in my face. "Why did you suspect the Prince's drink to be tainted? And I'd like you to be *very* specific. Tell me everything you can remember."

His attitude tells me that I was right about the champagne. But I have to keep playing dumb.

I can't blow my cover.

"Uh, well, like I told Juan, the waiter came out of the door and headed straight toward us. He only had one glass on his tray, which I thought was both odd and kinda rude, because I would have taken another glass. Mine wasn't actually empty, but it had gotten warm. When he presented it to the Prince, I thought maybe it was something special for him, but I didn't remember him ordering anything. It's like the first thing they teach girls of a certain age, never drink something you didn't pour or order yourself. Which, obviously, only really relates to party and club drinks because I have been drinking champagne off silver platters since I got here. It's just that the platters always come out full, and the waiters always wear white gloves, not black ones like this guy had. Really, it was the black gloves that gave me pause. And then when he walked straight out the other door. I'm sorry if I caused a scene. I didn't mean to. I highly doubt anyone would want to roofie the Prince." I laugh. "Well, except maybe for a few enthusiastic females who might want to bear a royal heir."

"Describe the man."

I try to make my description sound normal. Wordy. Not like a rap sheet. "Uh, he was shorter than me in heels, so like five-ten, maybe. He had short blond hair, light skin. There was a tattoo peeking out of his collar, but I couldn't see the design. He looked like he could have been of Slavic descent, maybe."

"Your brother, Ari, chased a man of that description. He and your driver fought and managed to subdue the man until the authorities came and took him into custody."

"So what did you find out?" Lorenzo asks.

"Nothing, other than that he is Russian," the admiral replies.

"Russian? First a German and a Moroccan, now a Russian? What, is the whole world out to get me?" the Prince asks. "Did you question him? Find out who he is working for?"

"We did not. He killed himself with the same poison found in your glass, a cyanide salt compound. You would have been dead within minutes." He turns to me. "You have done a great service to our country, Miss Von

Allister. We cannot thank you enough."

Both the Prince's and my eyes widen as the Admiral and Juan leave the room.

The Prince gives my hand a squeeze. "It seems I owe you my life again. If you keep this up, I'm going to have to hire you as a bodyguard."

I press my free hand against his chest. "You do have a nice body, from what I've heard."

He leans in and gives me a steamy kiss, but we are interrupted by his mother, who bursts through the door.

"Lorenzo, darling, I just heard." She sees us kissing. "Oh, excuse me."

"It's okay, Mother," he says, pulling his lips away from mine. "I was just thanking Huntley for saving me yet again."

"I've made a decision. I'm cancelling the Queen's Ball."

"You can't. We cannot allow our nation's activities to be dictated by fear."

"I know you are right, but there have been two attempts on your life in as many days. I don't want you attending any more parties. We'll say you are ill."

"I appreciate your concern, Mother, but I'll be fine." He gives her a hug.

"What about the charity race tomorrow?" she asks.

"I must," Lorenzo firmly states.

"You have nearly been gunned down and poisoned,"

she argues.

"This is my country. If I can't feel safe and free to go about my business, neither will our countrymen. They will lose faith in the monarchy."

"So you'd rather they lose the future of their country? Lose you?"

"This country is bigger than one man."

Although technically I agree with Lorenzo, I have to side with his mom on this one. "Um," I interrupt. "I know nothing about security stuff, but I can think of a million ways the charity race could go wrong."

"Like what?" He smiles, patronizing me.

"Another driver crashing into you, someone tampering with your car, tacks on the track to blow out your tires resulting in a fiery crash. The list could go on and on."

He hasn't rolled his eyes yet, but I'm getting the feeling neither his mother nor I are going to be able to talk any sense into him. And since I can't go in the car with him, I need to make sure he doesn't compete, so I go with the only option I have left and pull out the emotional card.

He's still holding my hand, so I give it a squeeze then turn to face him. "I don't want your mother, your country, or your father to watch you die."

"My father?"

"A television is being brought in," his mother confirms. It was a wild guess on my part, but I may have gotten lucky. "He wants to watch all the live footage. If he watched you die, it would kill him."

"He's already close to death," Lorenzo states sadly.

"Fine," I sputter out. "*I* don't want to watch you die."

He sighs, slides his arm around my waist, and gazes into my eyes. I take his face in my hands and give him a single kiss.

A kiss with more feeling than any kiss I've given him before. I keep my lips pressed against his for a long time. Our eyes are closed and our bodies still. It's intimate—all we can hear is the sound of our own hearts beating. Our kiss reminds me of when I'm in yoga class searching for inner peace. For me, it's illusive, because whenever I relax, I see my mother's face.

But in this moment, I know what it feels like—a strength and peace within yourself.

I open my eyes and whisper, "I care for you deeply, Lorenzo." I'm not pretending or manipulating. I truly mean every word.

Surprise appears in his eyes. I'm sure a lot of women have expressed their feelings for him, but he seems surprised that I have. So is his mother, who I almost forgot was in the room.

And, honestly, so am I.

AFTER HE AGREES not to participate in the charity race, I feign exhaustion and am driven home. He gives me a lengthy kiss when he walks me to my door. I rake my hands through the curls at the nape of his neck, deepening the kiss and enjoying the feel of his hands roaming across my backside.

By the time I shut the door, it's nearly three in the morning.

I strip down, put on my robe, and go sit on the terrace for a moment while trying to assimilate today's events. From what I've learned about the Terra Project to the attempts on the Prince's life. The fact that, so far, I've managed to keep him alive. But at this rate, if we don't figure out quickly who is behind the attempts, one will eventually succeed.

And I don't want that.

For a lot of reasons.

A glint in the corner of the balcony catches my eye. I investigate, finding an old-fashioned flip phone. I discover a note hidden inside that simply says, *Call Me.*

I take the phone into my closet and grab one of the makeup wipes I was given by the Kates that tests for bomb residue, and glide it over the phone, just in case, then take it down to the basement lab and analyze it.

Once I determine it's clean, I go back on my terrace and call the only stored number.

"Huntley?" a voice I immediately recognize as Terrance's says.

"Yeah?"

"I'm going to ask you a question, and I want your honest answer."

"Okay."

"Did you know your parents were spies before we talked the other day?"

"No, I did not."

"So do you think your parents wanted you to find out eventually?"

"I don't know."

"How did you get the watch? Did your dad give it to you?"

"No. The Dean of Blackwood Academy gave it to me about a month after I got there. I've worn it every day since. It's all I have left of him."

"And the locket?"

"No one knows about the locket. My mom gave it to me right before she died."

"What happened to your parents?"

"My mother was shot in front of me. Dad died by a car bomb. I got out."

"Then what?"

"I was sent to Blackwood."

"Immediately?"

"A week later."

"What's really on the memory card from the locket?"

"I don't know yet. I've been too busy trying to protect the Prince to find out."

"What were your parents' names?"

"Blake and Charlotte Cassleberry."

"And your real name?"

"I'd tell you, but I'd have to kill you."

"Funny."

"Fine. My name was Calliope Ann Cassleberry."

"I think they wanted you to know, eventually."

"Who wanted me to know what? And why?"

He doesn't reply, just says, "Can you sneak out tonight and meet me?"

"You're still in town?"

"Of course, I am."

"Aren't you glad you didn't chip me now, Terrance?" I tease.

"The fitness room at my hotel is open twenty-four seven. There will be a keycard sitting outside. Meet me there in ten minutes. And take off your watch."

"Why?"

"It has a tracking device in it. I didn't remove it."

"So someone has been keeping an eye on me all this time?"

"I think they could be."

I PULL A jacket over a workout bra and yoga pants, leave my watch under my pillow, throw on a ball cap, and exit through my terrace door.

The night is chilly, and you can practically taste the salt in the air.

With the moon lighting my short jog to the hotel, I get there quickly.

I use the key card to let myself in the hotel and am sure to tuck my head down so that my face is hidden from the security cameras in the hall, find the gym, and hop on an elliptical. My mind is going faster than the machine.

Fifty-two minutes later, Terrance finally shows up. He takes off his jacket, revealing a tank top and surprisingly buff arms and then gets on the elliptical next to me.

"You're late."

"I wanted to make sure neither of us was being followed. And I did some digging, for your parents' files and for yours."

"And?"

"When I searched your name—have you ever done that?"

"No."

"So you don't know that the Cassleberry family—including their twelve-year-old daughter—were all killed in a car accident six years ago?"

"What?" He shows me the article. "Did they fake my death to keep me safe?"

"Maybe. What did your dad tell you after your mom

was killed?"

"That something bad happened with their company. That we were going to leave the country. When we got in the car, it wouldn't start. He told me to get out of the car and run—and no matter what—not to stop running until I got to Uncle Sam's apartment. That he would take care of me."

"Uncle Sam?"

"He was a guy my dad was friends with. He wasn't my real uncle, but he lived a few blocks from my dad's office in a converted warehouse."

He stares at me. "As in the government, Uncle Sam?"

"I never even thought of that," I say, rubbing my temples. "Terrance, I'm on my first mission. I can't deal with all of this now."

"Tell me about how your mother was killed."

"It was just after dusk on a Wednesday night. I had been outside sitting up in a tree I liked to climb when she called me inside—weird, I just remembered that. Anyway, we were getting ready for bed when she heard a noise coming from the living room. She told me to hide in the closet, took the locket from around her neck, told me it was top secret, and that no matter what I heard I was not to come out. But then she screamed and I somehow knew she was in danger, so I got a gun out of my father's bedside table. I knew how to shoot, but I didn't plan to. I guess I thought I could give her the gun.

Or maybe use it to threaten whoever was there." I close my eyes, reliving it. "When I got to the living room, there was a man holding a gun to her head. He was yelling at her. Telling her to give him something. She had her head down, but was completely calm when she said she didn't have it. He slapped her. Told her she was going to die. She looked up and into the man's eyes, and that's when she noticed me standing behind him. She held my eyes and imperceptibly shook her head. I knew she wanted me to hide. I knew she didn't want him to see me. Her eyes were pleading. The man threatened her again and his finger twitched. I screamed. Pulled the trigger. Shot him in the shoulder. But it was too late. He had fired and I watched as a little round hole formed in her forehead."

"Then what?" he asks, startling me and causing me to open my eyes.

"He turned around and pointed his gun at me. I'll never forget the shape of his gun. It was a suppressed Beretta Twenty-One Bobcat pistol—I learned that later at school. They had them at the shooting range."

"Keep going."

"Oh, yeah. Um, then the rest is sort of a blur. I shot at him again, hit his arm and caused him to drop the gun. He lunged at me and knocked the gun out of my hand. I grabbed a long bamboo pole out of a decorative pot, used it as a weapon. I was already well-trained in martial arts. I hit his shoulder, which was bleeding all over the place. Then hit him in the head. He fell down. I dropped the stick and ran. He grabbed my foot as I ran by and knocked me to the floor. I managed to kick him in the face and got out of the house. He followed me, yelled at me to stop, that he just wanted to talk. But I didn't stop. I ran as fast as I could down the street. He fired at me. Missed. I think I ducked behind a car, because I remember glass from the window raining down. Then I ran into the neighbor's yard, jumped the fence, ran down an alley and out to the main thoroughfare, where I stole a coat from a chair outside a cafe and calmly walked the two miles to my father's office."

"Then what?"

"I was bleeding. Someone patched me up. When my dad got there, I told him everything that had happened, minus the necklace part. He hugged me. We stayed at his office. I slept a lot and he worked a lot. We didn't really talk about my mom. Didn't have a funeral. Or a memorial. Forty-eight hours later, we got in his car. He told me we were leaving the country for a while. When he turned the ignition, the car made a weird sputtering sound. He looked scared, told me to get out. Go to Uncle Sam's. I jumped out, the car exploded. I was knocked to the ground and dinged up, but I ran to Uncle Sam's. The same person bandaged me up. I stayed there. A week later, I was at Blackwood."

"And you've never told anyone about the necklace?"

"No."

"Did anyone ask you if your mom gave you anything?"

"Both my dad and Uncle Sam did, but I told them no. I thought she wanted me to keep it a secret. Like it was meant just for me because it had our picture in it— never once did I think she literally meant *top secret*, as in classified."

"Let's take a look."

"I'm not sure I should let you, Terrance. She may have died for this."

"You have to trust someone. I have more to show you."

"You show me yours, I'll show you mine?" I tease.

HE GRINS AT me and leads me into an empty relaxation room, grabbing a bottle of water out of the mini fridge along the way and tossing it to me.

"I have a hacker friend who is here in Montrovia working on something top secret."

"Something related to the Prince?"

"He couldn't tell me. Anyway, he can get into anything—anytime, anywhere. He had never heard of Blackwood Academy either, but he was able to find it and then through a series of sophisticated techniques—"

"Terrance, I need facts, not how you did it."

"Well, it was brilliant. Double back door, password, encryption. Anyway, we hacked into Blackwood and found your file. You're a badass, by the way. And they definitely knew you were sneaking out. In fact, they kept making it harder for you. They were testing you."

"Obviously, I passed. And no offense, but I hacked into my own file. Actually, one of the guys I dated—"

"Hooked up with?"

"Whatever—hacked it for me."

"You only saw what they wanted you to see. Basic notes about your behavior. Your personality profile. Notes from your shrink and teachers. Your grades. Right?"

"Yes. So what did you find out?"

"That Blackwood didn't exist before you. I believe it may have been *created* for you."

"That makes no sense. The school had been there forever. I was the new kid."

"It had only been there for a week. For years before that, Blackwood had been an elite boarding school, but the school was relocated suddenly *due to toxic mold*." He studies me. "Have you ever thought that your parents were training you to be a spy? You speak how many languages? Your passport has more stamps than anyone I know."

"But why?"

"That's what I want to know. I also wanted to know

about your partner—your brother, Ari—how was he chosen. And why. We were able to access his CIA file, no problem."

"What did you find out about him?"

"Father was a big deal, stationed at the Pentagon. His son went to military school and then was sent to train with the CIA. That was unusual, but given his family background it makes sense that they would make an exception. What *is* surprising is that you have *no* file."

I shrug. "I probably don't warrant one yet."

He shakes his head, disagreeing. "With the way your parents died, there should be something. The CIA is meticulous at recording information. We did find something interesting, though. An encrypted message. Just five words. Sent to an address we couldn't trace."

"What did it say?"

"*Spy Girl is a go.* It went out on Sunday morning at 11:12 a.m. Eastern Standard Time."

"The Dean called me into his office at 10:30 to give me my mission."

"I think *you* are Spy Girl."

I can't help but smile. "I have a code name?"

"Yes," he says, punching me in the shoulder. "Don't look so happy. Tell me this, when did you first hear the name Huntley Bond?"

"A few days ago, when I was given my mission."

"There are Huntley Bond social media accounts.

Well, Huntley Bond-Von Allister now—you recently announced your name change."

"I what?" He pulls up a profile and scrolls through photos of me over the years. "I don't understand. These are my photos, but at Blackwood we weren't allowed on social media. We had our own private intranet they called XBook. It allowed us to post stuff for each other to see and chat with each other after curfew, but was not public."

"My guess is they allowed you to post on XBook, then some were filtered through to here. Look, a few weeks ago when Ares Von Allister passed, you mentioned a life-changing event. They've been setting up your cover for months. Years. Six years, to be exact."

He pulls up a post where I mention finding out about my real father and the brother I never knew. Along with a cute selfie. Since then, no posts.

"Part of me is mad I didn't know about this. Part of me thinks it's brilliant. Have they done this for all the Blackwood students?"

"I wondered the same thing myself. So I compared the students from the Blackwood intranet to what was out there. The answer is no. It's like the rest of the students don't exist. There were no real names in their files, only letters of the alphabets. And I have a sneaking suspicion that the reclusive Ares Von Allister's death was well-timed."

"You think he was murdered?"

"I think we have to consider that possibility. His passing was essential to your cover."

"That's what doesn't make sense. After today, I won't ever be able to go undercover again. I was photographed with the Queen. Why would they spend all this time training and cover building to blow it on saving the Prince of one small country?"

"You tell me, Spy Girl." He looks at his watch. "I gotta go, and you need sleep, Huntley Penelope Bond-Von Allister." He hands me the small duffle that he brought in. "There's a phone in here. I added a little technology, so it's untraceable. Destroy the other one and only use this to call me if you need something important. The number is saved. It will route it to a computer, and I will receive the message. Be careful. I have a feeling you're being watched very closely."

"Because they have high expectations?"

"That and because I think it's a little too much of a coincidence that Blackwood is now closing its doors."

"It is?"

"Yes, and there's something else." He glances nervously around the room, like he's afraid to tell me.

"What?"

"A few minutes after we read your file, it was deleted. Actually, *all* the files were gone. Like Blackwood never existed. Like *you* never existed."

I shake my head not even sure how to reply to this information. I just give Terrance a hug. As I do, I hand him the disk from my mom's locket. "This may put you in danger."

"I can handle it."

"How do I know you're not part of whatever scheme this is?"

"You don't, Spy Girl. But you have to trust some-one."

MISSION: DAY SIX

AFTER MY MEETING with Terrance, I snuck back into my room and quickly fell asleep. I'm awakened a few hours later by Ari.

"We need to talk."

"About what?"

"Our mission, duh."

"Oh, sorry. Not really awake yet."

"This can't be helped. With the Prince constantly at your side, it doesn't give us time to talk. Ellis said you requested information on the cousins and their boyfriends. I have that info and have been over it." He drops a file in my lap. "Read it and destroy it."

"You want to give me the condensed version? Is there anything you thought was pertinent?"

"I think it's important we both read it. There may be

something you catch that I don't. You read. I'll order breakfast. What sounds good?"

"Don't laugh, but I'm dying for a cheeseburger. And hash browns."

"Done," he says, picking up the phone and ordering us two, along with a couple fully-caffeinated sodas.

He sits on my bed, messing around on his phone, while I read.

"I heard you slept with Allie again."

"Because she snuck into my bedroom the night they arrived. Last night, I was working on getting close to Clarice."

"How did that go?"

"It didn't. But I did get the impression that it might, tonight."

I keep reading, nothing catching my attention until . . . "Wait, their father was killed six months ago? In a hunting *accident* that may have been a suicide? Wouldn't he have been in line for the throne after Lorenzo?"

"Yes, he was."

"What are you thinking?"

"Well, here's an interesting little tidbit to go along with that. The accident happened just a few days before I was pulled out of school and sent to train with the CIA, or whoever it is that I'm working for."

"You don't think we're working for the CIA?" I ask.

"I'm starting to wonder if it's something more. One

of those organizations that is more covert."

"Like we could be working for the bad guys?"

"No, but I get the feeling they operate outside of the usual boundaries."

"Does the CIA have boundaries?"

"You tell me. You were trained for this, too," he says, and I realize he doesn't know about Black X. And it makes me wonder about them—who they are and what they do. I try to remember where I first heard about them. It comes back clear as day. Sitting in the Dean's office—talking about my future—he told me about an agency so covert even the President didn't know of its existence. He told me it was small, elite, and powerful. And that they would understand my need for revenge. It immediately became my goal. My focus. To be good enough for them to want me. Because deep down I knew that the CIA would probably not allow me to go rogue and kill my mother's assassin.

"You're right. It feels a little different—but I think it may be due to the excess."

"How is it any different from them buying infor-mation in the Middle East after the Gulf Wars? They supposedly had bags full of millions of U.S. dollars. All for info."

"Maybe this is the new CIA?"

"Yeah, maybe. So back to the cousins," Ari says. "Do you think they could have killed their own father?"

"Ophelia is bossy, but I think she's harmless."

"I'd say the same thing about Viktor."

"He's part Russian, though. Just like the guy who tried to poison the Prince last night. Do we know anything about him yet?"

"Mercenary," Ari says. "Works for the highest bidder. Just like the gunmen."

"None of whom have lived to enjoy their money. Do you think that will mean others will be less likely to try?"

"I expect the ante to be even higher. Although our government has picked up nothing relating to this."

"So three dead ends and we're back to where we started."

"Not really. I think we have to focus our efforts on Clarice."

"She just seems so sweet. Annoying as hell, but I just don't picture her killing people. She doesn't want animals to die."

"Maybe she doesn't feel the same way about people? And you can't dismiss the fact that she may want to make the Terra Project come to life here in Montrovia."

"Which means she'd not only kill her father, her cousin, and her sister, but she'd kill the monarchy, too."

He nods.

"What do we know about the cousins' life? About their relationship with their father? And where is their mother? Was she not at the Queen's party?"

"That's further into the file," Ari states. "Their parents were only briefly married. After an ugly divorce, their mother moved them to France. They lived comfortably but were not raised with the same affluence as Lorenzo."

"So how do they feel about him?"

"Maybe that's something you should ask them. When Clarice turned eighteen, both girls moved into their father's Montrovian mansion."

"What do we know about the boyfriend?"

"Well, if we're right about her father's death being connected, the fact that she met him only a few weeks ago rules him out, right?"

"I suppose, but I still don't like him. Something about him makes the hair on the back of my neck stand up."

"He's from France—mother is French, father is Albanian. He was arrested for protesting at a global climate conference once, but other than that his record is clean."

"Did they know each other before they started dating?"

"He told me they only recently met."

"Here's a theoretical question. What happens if Clarice were to succeed in becoming Queen? If she tried to change the country dramatically, wouldn't the military protest? The people protest?"

"I suspect all would be done for the good of the

country and before they knew it things would be very different in Montrovia."

"But I thought that Montrovia is geographically important because of all the oil transported on its waters? I thought that was why our government is worried. Even the Saudis are worried based on what Lorenzo said. I mean, that's the real reason we are here, right? Because our country and our allies don't want the Strait to fall into the wrong hands."

"Think about it. If Clarice succeeds, there will be no military. Based on her comments about green living and fossil fuels, I'm thinking stopping the flow of oil through her country's waters might be one of the first things she would do."

Our conversation is interrupted by our breakfast being brought to my room. Ellis follows the server in and hands me the local morning newspaper.

"I'm on the front page?" I ask in shock.

"You're on page six, as well. There are numerous photos on the Internet of you and Prince Lorenzo together. You're famous, my dear," Ellis states.

After the server gets our breakfast set up and leaves, I hand Ellis the file Ari gave me and ask him to destroy it. Along with the newspaper.

If this keeps up, I may have no choice but to become a princess.

I DECIDE TO spend the rest of the morning shopping, specifically for something spectacular to wear tonight. Yes, the Kates sent some beautiful dresses and basics, but I'm looking for something sinfully short, sexy, and sparkly.

I find it at the second store I visit. The staff is extremely helpful, possibly due to the fact that I was on the front page this morning.

But as I move from store to store, I realize that I'm being followed by a man wearing a ball cap. I use a few simple evasion tactics without being obvious, not to lose him, but just to verify that he is, in fact, following me. I try one more technique. One a little more advanced, but the man is not tricked. When I come out of the alley, I stop to look in a store window, a crude but effective touch of tradecraft, which allows me to see that he's still behind me.

And I know instantly that this man is not paparazzi looking for a picture. So why is he following me? Does he think I'm going to meet the Prince? Or is he interested in me?

I pop into a store to see if he will follow me and make myself look at a few evening bags. I'm trying to decide if I should buy a pricey clutch for tonight when he enters the store, walks straight up to me, and says, "You should have that."

The fact that he's this close has me on edge. I back

up a little so I have more space to maneuver should he pull out a weapon.

"You think?" I ask, playing dumb, putting the skinny chain on my shoulder and studying myself in the mirror, while discreetly tapping my heel to expose the blade. "I can't decide if I should get it."

"I think you should." He takes off his ball cap and holds out his hand. "I'm William Gallagher."

Holy smokes!

It can't be.

I don't know what this man's real name is—no one does—but I certainly know his code name, Intrepid. He's a British spy. A freaking legend. I should know. I studied his body of work for my senior dissertation. We were given old case studies and classified files to work with. I saw a few grainy photos of him and was smitten. The combination of his expertise and his classic good looks made him my ultimate spy crush. Meeting him is like a fantasy, and I'm dying to ask him if the accounts I read are true. Like did he really jump out of a van traveling fifty miles per hour and onto the car of a rogue agent—who was going to sell a flash drive with a list of all the undercover British Intelligence agents on it—and then shot him through the roof? And what about the time he supposedly hung from the base of a helicopter while it was flying and managed to board it, take control, and defuse the bomb they were about to drop onto

Buckingham Palace? I also want to ask if he really retired. It seems odd that he did, since he's only in his thirties.

Did I mention he's extremely handsome? If they were to cast my perfect spy in a movie, it would be this guy. I can picture him buying a dress for a beautiful girl and then taking her to the casino and always having time for sex, even though he's in the middle of a mission. It's probably the reason why he is an expert at recruiting people to help his cause. I know the key to his success is charm combined with deadliness. Compassionate eyes that hide a cold killer. A body made for long hours of sinful sex, and a face that belongs on a statue.

I'm so enthralled by his presence, I can't do anything other than smile at him. It's not like I can go all fan girl and tell him I admire his work. Particularly, the job he did in Northern Ireland, where he alone killed seventeen men who were working in a farmhouse creating a car bomb that they planned to detonate at the Summer Olympics.

"Do you have a name?" he finally asks, making me feel like a moron.

"Oh, yeah. I'm, uh, Huntley. Huntley Bond. I mean, Huntley Von Allister."

"I saw you with Prince Lorenzo last night at the fashion show. And with the Vice President's son at the Smithsonian Gala. You run with a pretty influential crowd."

"Sounds like you've been hanging out at the same places as I have, yet we've never met."

"Are you and Daniel close?"

"We met when we were seated at the same table at the gala, and he introduced me to the Prince a few days ago."

"I heard about your father, Ares, may he rest in peace. Funny, I didn't know he had children."

"Neither did I until I was contacted by an attorney. To say I was shocked, is an understatement." I study the clutch in my hand. "And even though I can easily afford this now and am absolutely in love with it, I'm having a hard time spending the money. I have a party to go to tonight, and it would look adorable with my dress, but it's not very practical."

"Can a four thousand euro evening bag ever be considered practical?" he jokes.

I scrunch up my nose. "You're right. I shouldn't get it."

"The party you are going to tonight. Would that be the one on the team owner's yacht?"

I almost answer yes. But then stop.

He supposedly retired. What if he's not working for the British anymore? What if he's become a hit man, working only for the highest bidder? And what if he's here to assassinate the Prince?

It would really, really suck if I had to kill this man. I

briefly wonder if I could sleep with him first.

"I'm not sure where we're going. I was just told to dress hot."

"I also heard you're throwing a party in your lovely villa."

"You've heard an awful lot. Been reading the tabloids?"

He smiles at me and shakes his head. "I'm friends with Wesley. He mentioned both you and your upcoming party. I was sort of hoping he would get me an invitation."

"He hasn't even asked."

"I guess he's not a very good friend."

"Apparently not. Nice to meet you, William. I have to go," I say, then hightail myself back home.

I'M JUST PULLING into the villa gates when I get a call from the Prince.

"What are you doing right this second?"

"Just getting home. What are *you* doing right this second?"

"Thinking about you in a bikini."

"For our bath time?"

"It's a lovely day. What would you think about spending the afternoon on my yacht watching the charity races? You can have your household staff deliver the bath bombs to the palace."

"I'm pretty sure if I send any kind of bomb to the palace, I will get arrested. Maybe we should call them fizzies."

"Very well, then. Bath fizzies—although I'm partial to the name bath bombs. Way more intrigue. Have them delivered along with whatever you need to get ready for this evening to my residence."

"I have hair and makeup appointments."

"Send them to the palace."

"Um, okay. It's a date."

"Perfect. Can you be ready in five minutes? I am quite possibly on the way to your villa as we speak."

I SHOUT ORDERS to Ellis as I run to my room. I quickly change into a bikini then prepare to pack a tote with essentials. Then I realize I have no idea what to pack.

"Ari!" I yell out in a panic.

He comes rushing into my room, gun first, eyes sweeping the area.

"What are you doing?"

"The way you screamed, I thought you were in danger."

"Danger of looking stupid on the Royal Yacht. What the heck does one wear on a yacht? Do you have any idea? The Kates didn't brief us on that." He sighs for a long moment. "Sorry, I scared you. Oh, shit. I almost forgot. You'll never, ever believe who I met at the store today. Who I'm pretty sure was following me, and who I'm pretty sure wants to come to our party before the race."

"Who?"

"William Gallagher."

"Should I know that name?"

I crinkle my brow. "It's probably not his real name, but I do know that he's one of the most revered British intelligence agents in, like maybe, all of history. His code name is Intrepid."

"Never heard of him. Why would he want to come to our party? Why would he follow you?"

"I'm not sure. Supposedly, he retired. But that's weird because he's not that old. So I'm torn between he's become a paid assassin and wants to kill the Prince, or he's working for his government and wants to save him."

"Interesting. You don't think he knows that *we* work for the government, do you?"

"He did mention he never knew Ares had children. He seemed skeptical. But then he was sort of flirting with me. He said he knows Wesley."

"While you go to the harbor, I'll have Housekeeping do some digging. I think they are busy planning our party, but this is important."

"Let me know what you find out. Send me a heart if he's a good guy and a broken heart if he's bad. And pray for a heart, because I will be crushed if I have to kill him."

Ari chuckles but then looks at me seriously. "Do you think you are good enough to kill a legend?"

"Retired legend," I clarify. "And the answer to that question is absolutely." I hear a car rumble into the drive. "Lorenzo is here. Shit."

Ari speaks to his phone, asking it what to wear on a yacht in Montrovia. Numerous example photos pop up. "Designer heels and sunglasses with a teeny bikini." He scrolls through more photos while I pull on a pair of white shorts and a navy sweater over my swimsuit.

"Perfect," Ari says.

"What are you doing today?"

He doesn't reply, so I grab my bag and go to greet Lorenzo.

Ari follows me and says to him, "Huntley said you'll be on your yacht this afternoon. Does that mean the two of you aren't going to your cousins' spur of the moment beach party?"

Lorenzo lowers his voice. "They wanted to have it on my boat and are a little miffed that I said no."

"Why did you say no?" I ask.

"Because I wanted to spend time alone with you."

I smile because Lorenzo is so sweet. Ari smiles because he knows this is good for our mission.

LORENZO DRIVES US to the harbor, a blacked-out SUV

following us closely. The race traffic is bad as many streets are closed, but Lorenzo pulls through a parking garage and emerges at the marina. He parks, and we are escorted to his boat.

After taking off my shoes, I get a tour of his amazing yacht. It sports a navy steel hull with a white superstructure on top and is curvy like a racecar. The interior is made up of rich woods accented in stainless steel with lots of leather upholstery. It's a combination of sleek, rich, contemporary warmth. It has six staterooms for guests as well as a massive owner's suite and room for a large crew. It also features five levels of sundecks, a pool, nightclub, and numerous entertaining salons.

"It's one of the prettiest boats in the harbor," I tell him as we go to the top deck to view the charity races.

"Thank you. My father would love to hear you say that."

"Why's that?"

"He worked with Viktor's father's yacht company over the last two years having it built for my twenty-third birthday."

"When was that?"

"In March, but it only finally arrived last week. You are my first guest."

"But I've seen pictures of you on yachts surrounded by women. There was one in the paper just the other day."

"Not on this boat. You are the first woman, besides my mother, to step foot on it."

"Well, I'm honored then."

"I thought we could have lunch up here and then enjoy the sun on the pool deck."

"That sounds perfect."

He gives me a kiss. "So, how is my beautiful Huntley today?"

"It seems she's on the cover of the newspaper."

"Yes, our publicist did mention that there are a lot of photos of us. Are you okay with that?"

I laugh. "Um, the question should be are you okay with that? I'm a nobody. No one cares who I'm with."

"I do," he says, kissing me again. "And I prefer you be photographed with me as opposed to another man. Did you remember to send the bombs to my house?"

"I did—not that you gave me much time—and you need to stop calling them that. I'll end up getting arrested."

"You may get arrested if anyone sees you in this," he teases, pulling a teeny white thong that looks too small for a Barbie doll out of his duffle bag. Good thing the Kates insisted on the Brazilian wax down there. "This is what you will be wearing."

"I'm not wearing that."

"It's for bath time, not for yacht time."

"Well, thank goodness."

I look around at all the boats in the harbor, each one packed to the gills with spectators. "Did you notice this is the only yacht not full of people watching the race?"

"I hadn't noticed. I only have eyes for you."

I laugh. "Really?"

"You talked me out of participating in the charity race. I'm not sure what kind of spell you have me under."

"Love potion, probably," I tease. "Ordered from Weasleys' Wizard Wheezes in Diagon Alley."

"Harry Potter," he says, doing a great imitation of Dobby the house elf, which causes me to burst out in laughter.

I stifle my laugh when a sommelier brings us a bottle of wine, allowing Lorenzo the opportunity to taste it and deem it good enough to drink.

He holds his glass up and touches mine. "Love is the beauty of the soul."

I recite the rest of the quote. "*Insomuch as love grows in you, so beauty grows. For love is the beauty of the soul.*"

"Do you believe that?" he asks, holding my gaze.

"I think love grows in us, but I don't think love is always beautiful." An image of my mother clouds my vision, but this time, instead of watching her head get blown away, I see her eyes before she got shot, full of love for me. Not caring about herself, only wanting to protect me at all costs. It saddens me to know that she died worried for me. I feel like I let her down.

Tears gather in my eyes.

"Huntley?" the Prince asks, searching my face.

"Sorry, the answer to your question is *yes*. I believe love to be a beautiful thing."

"Where did you just go?" he asks. I put my head down. I'm not supposed to let him in. I can't, but he gently touches my face. "Tell me."

"I was just thinking about my mother," I answer honestly.

"How old were you when she passed?"

"Twelve."

"And your father?"

"They both died then."

He sets his glass down without taking a drink and pulls me into his arms, kissing the top of my head, and hugging me. "I will admit to knowing all that, but I wanted to hear it from you."

"Let me guess, your security checked me out?"

"Yes."

"Is that normal protocol for everyone you date?"

"No, but it is for the girl who saved my life twice. I want to know everything about you. Is it bad that I read their report?"

"My life hasn't been very exciting, so I imagine it was a rather dull read."

"You are well-traveled. That was the most interesting

thing. Passport stamps from all over the world, even from a young age."

What he says gives me pause, because this was not in my backstory. But maybe my real story is my backstory, just with a different name. I realize that this is a do or die situation. If what I say and what he read in my file don't agree, he will know I'm lying, and I'll end up in a Montrovian jail—or worse, sent home a failure.

"My parents traveled a lot for their jobs, and we often stayed for months at a time," I reply, then quickly try to change the subject. "I particularly love visiting ruins and museums."

"You mentioned that at the castle. What do you like about them?"

"When you combine the literature and art from an era, you get a good idea of how people of different time periods lived. It's intriguing that at the core, their lives weren't all that different from ours. There was good and evil. Love and hate. War and peace. Happiness and tragedy. I find that comforting."

"How so?"

"Because someone else has probably gone through something similar to what I have, if not worse."

"We still haven't sealed our toast," he says, handing me back my glass. "To love worth recording."

"I'll drink to that," I say, feeling like I just dodged a very big bullet.

WE HAVE LUNCH then sit on the pool deck for a bit, enjoying each class of the charity races and then a practice session for the professionals.

We're cheering for his favorite driver, who is out on the track, when one of his security detail brings a wrapped package and sets it in front of me.

My immediate thought is that it's a bomb. I consider picking it up and throwing it into the bay, hoping it wouldn't destroy all these yachts. I must have a panicked look on my face because the man says, "It's a gift for you from a friend. We opened it, checked to make sure it was legitimate, and rewrapped it. Sorry, it's not quite as pretty as when it arrived."

"What is it?" Lorenzo asks as the guard retreats to his position.

"I have no idea." I carefully open the box and pray they properly vetted it. When I take the lid off, I find the Judith Leiber silver crystal clutch with red and pink lips that I was coveting at the store today. "Wow."

Lorenzo takes the card out of the box and reads it. "*You should never walk away from something you love, even if it's impractical.* It's signed with just a W. Do you know who that is?"

"I think so. William Gallagher. He was at the store when I was considering buying it."

"Is he British?"

"Yes. What do you know about him?" I try to make

the question sound curious and not like an interrogation.

"He works for the government."

"He was following me."

"Why?"

"I don't know. He asked me if we were going to the yacht party tonight, but I didn't give him an answer. It seemed weird, you know? After everything that's happened."

He calls Juan over and speaks to him discreetly. Then he says, "You have good instincts. You're very clever."

"Thank you. Um, do you think it's okay if I keep the clutch?"

He laughs. "Did you really love it and not buy it?"

"Yes."

"Then William and I are in agreement. You should have everything your heart desires, Huntley, my dear."

AFTER THE PRACTICE session concludes, we head to the castle to take our bath and prepare for the party tonight.

I put on the teeny white thong and find him waiting for me in a mini euro Speedo type thing. It doesn't leave much to the imagination.

I remind myself that topless is normal here and fight the urge to cover my boobs. And although the other night there was some over-the-dress boob action that went on, this is the first time Lorenzo has seen them naked. It's both awkward and stimulating.

He leads me into a palatial bathroom, which features a huge sunken tub large enough for a crowd. The water has been drawn. The bathroom glitters with ornate blue and gold metallic tiles and features a cathedral ceiling covered with paintings of mermaids, Greek gods, and elaborate sailing vessels—all supported by marble Doric-style columns.

"Are you ready to add the bath bombs?" he chuckles, holding up the bag.

"Why don't you do the honors?" I suggest, sitting on the edge and watching his expression as they bubble and fizz.

"The water is turning very blue," he says nervously.

"Don't worry." I grab the smaller bag of golden bars, get into the tub, and break them up under the faucet. "We won't go to the party looking like Smurfs."

He laughs. "That is a relief. Would you care for some champagne?"

"I'd love some," I reply as he pours me a glass. It's French, dry, and tastes expensive.

He steps into the bath, sits down, and we both relax. It's really quite nice, sitting close to him, mostly naked, all warm and sipping on champagne.

He wraps an arm around my shoulder, and I lean back into it.

"So are you only here for the week?" he asks.

"We leased the villa for a few months."

"Do you like it?"

"Are you kidding? It's beautiful."

"Would you ever consider settling in my great country?"

"I read Montrovia is very easy to visit, but living here is another story. Foreign real estate transactions must be approved by the government for anyone who isn't Montrovian by birth."

"You could always stay here."

"If you tell that to all the girls you date, there's probably a waiting list."

He chuckles, and it's clear I'm amusing him. "Would *you* like to?"

"I would like to, but I won't."

"Why not?"

"Because I'm not looking to be your nanny." I cup water in my hand and pour it onto his chest with a grin.

Which causes him to do the same to me, the warm water gliding through my cleavage.

"What about a princess?"

I laugh—choke, practically, on my champagne.

"Ohmigosh, that usually works, doesn't it? No wonder when I Googled your country all the images that came up were photos of you with different women. It seems tourism ranks second place by a mile."

He takes a sip of his champagne, looking thoughtful. Probably trying to figure out how to make himself sound less of a cad. I mean they call him the Playboy Prince for good reason.

"If the papers are correct, there may be a royal wedding soon," he says, finally, apparently deciding it's better to just change the subject.

"That stands to reason, since your cousin got engaged yesterday in a very public way."

"Why do I get the feeling you haven't read the papers or seen the articles about us?"

"Because I haven't. I saw the photo on the front cover of the local paper, and that was enough." I move away from him and swim across the pool-sized bath.

"Why?" he asks, following.

"I'm not sure hats are a good look for me. I looked awkward."

He pins me into the corner and kisses me. "You were beautiful. Did you get your invitation for tonight?"

"Ari said they were delivered while I was out this morning shopping for a dress."

"And did you find one?"

"That was the good thing about the photo in the paper. Everyone in the stores was very helpful. And I did."

"What does it look like?"

"What little there is of it is silver and fringy." He nuzzles his face into my neck then slowly kisses his way to my mouth. I honestly fully expected I'd have to fend him off today, but he's behaving very well.

Although part of me wishes he wouldn't. I'm torn between my own desire and what I deem to be good for my mission.

I move onto the Prince's lap. He smiles and wraps his arms around me and continues talking. I'm thinking that he doesn't usually talk much to the girls he sleeps with. It helps that conversation flows easily between us.

"Before we go, I have to meet with the Saudi Prince again. He says his country is still concerned about our shipping lanes allowing him passage to Europe."

"Why?" I ask, running my hands gently through his hair. I need to get his take on it all. I also wonder what the Saudis have heard that has made them nervous. "Is he a friend?"

Lorenzo squints, an imperceptible twitch that tells me *no*—regardless of what comes out of his mouth next.

"He feels our military is lacking, but we have controlled the Strait for over four hundred years," he says, suddenly holding up his hand and studying it. "My hand is gold."

"I'll take all the glitter, so I will sparkle tonight." I laugh, taking his hands and rubbing them down my arm. "I can see why the Prince is worried, though, things have changed in the world."

He glances at the clock letting me know that bath time is over, so we swim over to where the towels are.

"Yes, terrorism is an unfortunate side effect—"

"I've never really understood that," I say, wrapping a fluffy towel around me. He does the same, and we sit on a bench and continue to talk.

"Terrorism? Extremism?"

"Yeah. I mean look through a history book. People have been killing each other for centuries in the name of religion, and I don't get it. Nearly every religion teaches peace. Man's ability to twist whatever gospel they believe—is where we get into trouble. People laugh at pageant contestants who say they want world peace, but isn't that what we should all want?"

"All you need is love? Do you believe that?"

"If we truly loved our fellow man, yeah, I do. Have you ever heard of the Terra Project?"

"No. Wait, yes. Clarice was speaking of it the other night. But I don't know what it is all about."

I give him an overview.

"Interesting concept, but it wouldn't work. You'd still need currency to barter with and a government to back that currency. Plus, I like my life the way it is."

To prove his point, his phone dings on the table next to me. I pick it up and hand it to him, noticing the text that says: *My kitty misses you* and is followed by a photo—of which you can assume is *not* her cat.

I laugh, goofily. Who the hell in the basement of Black X ever thought I had a chance in hell of capturing the Prince's attention when cooter pics are sent to him daily?

"Friend or acquaintance?" I ask.

He tilts his head, considering. "Acquaintance, who *wants* to be a friend."

"More like a princess. I bet that sucks, though, sometimes—having women throw themselves at you."

He tries not to smile. It's clear he doesn't agree. "Isn't it every man's fantasy?" he asks, taking another sip of champagne.

"I suppose, but what if it's like anything you gorge on? Eventually, you lose your taste for it—or worse, grow to hate it. It would really be a shame if you lost the taste for kitty."

He blows champagne out of his mouth, laughing. "You are funny." He caresses my hair. "Would you like to be the one I gorge on?"

I back away. "I'd rather gorge on love, because that's the one thing you never get sick of."

"Hopeless romantic?"

"Maybe."

"Yet, your first night in Montrovia you went home with a British lad you had just met."

"How would you know that?"

"He talks. Says you're wild."

"Wesley was so drunk, he passed out before any wildness could take place," I lie. In reality, I may have shot him with a tranquilizer dart and drug him to bed.

"You spent the night. When he woke up, you were naked."

"No, I was wearing *exactly* what I'm wearing now—albeit, a larger version. Basically, I was wearing what one would to the beach in your lovely country."

"You were in an evening gown at the casino."

"Which was entirely sequined. I would have ruined the dress had I slept in it."

"So, he lied?"

"Well, I may have led him to believe we'd had a good night."

"Why?"

"Before I realized he was shit-faced, he was sweet to me."

"How so?"

"I was at the bar and someone made a nasty comment about my dress. He told the guy to shut up. It was chivalrous, and I appreciate that in a man."

"Sounds like you need a prince."

"Oh, for gosh sake, give it a rest. You're the Prince. I get it. If I succumb to his royal sexual wishes, maybe I could live a fairytale. No thanks."

"No thanks?" He's taken aback.

I lean toward him, my towel purposely slipping a little in the front. "Lorenzo, if all I wanted to do was screw you, I would have already."

"You were straddling me in the mermaid bath," he counters. "And you said you care about me in front of my mother."

"I'm not saying I'm not attracted to you, but when you drop all the prince shit and be yourself, I really like you. You're funny. Smart. Interesting to talk to. I enjoy your company."

For this I get a grin. "I enjoy your company, too. I've had a lovely day and am looking forward to a wonderful evening." He glances at the clock again. "I'm supposed to be there in ten minutes."

"Then, I'll have to join you later. I'm afraid it'll take longer than that for me to get ready. Hair and makeup isn't due for another twenty minutes."

"I took the liberty of acquiring the dress from the fashion show for you to wear to the Queen's Ball."

"So I'd sleep with you?"

He grins and pulls me closer. "Huntley, if all I wanted to do was screw you, I would have already."

I swallow hard as my body heats up again. He says it like a threat as he holds a robe out for me. I slide off the wet bottoms, gently rub the plush towel across my skin to dry it, and then drop it to the floor—allowing him a full shot of me naked—before slipping into the robe.

As he grabs the belt and securely cinches it around my waist, he sighs heavily, acting as if it is the only thing keeping us apart.

He strips out of his euro-Speedo, eyes me—and wraps a towel around his waist, shielding himself from my view.

And I know without a doubt I'm going to have to sleep with him soon.

HE GOES TO his meeting while I get ready. Along with my dress for tonight, there is a box adorned with an elaborately embroidered silk. Inside is a credit card to allow me entry—and probably to prevent people from crashing—along with a scroll declaring the party details. It's quite luxe, and I've never seen an invitation like it.

After my hair and makeup are complete, I get dressed and then go into the billiards room and play darts to pass the time.

"Remind me to never play with you," Lorenzo says, entering the room and eyeing my score, which consists of five bulls-eyes and one just outside ring. "You're a ringer."

"No, I never lie about my dart throwing abilities," I tease.

"You look gorgeous. That is quite the dress."

"You don't think it's too scandalous?"

"I love a good scandal," he says, pulling me into his arms and kissing my neck.

THE PARTY IS ridiculous. The yacht is worth at least three

hundred million dollars and is decked out in more of the embroidered silk from the invitations. The guests are all A-list, with royalty, celebrities, drivers, and more beautiful people and designer clothing than I have ever seen in one place. The security is tight, and I find myself relaxing and just enjoying the atmosphere and my date, who holds my hand and adorably introduces me to everyone he knows.

I haven't seen Ari since we arrived, but he did send me a text earlier. It was just a heart, meaning that Gallagher is one of the good guys.

I'm returning from a quick trip to the ladies' room when I run smack dab into the British spy. The hallway is narrow, and he makes it feel tighter by placing his hand above the wall near my shoulder and leaning toward me.

"I saw you on the Royal Yacht in your bikini today. The French Barbie twins on the neighboring boat were jealous."

"Because I was alone with the Prince?"

"Mostly because of how you looked in your bikini."

I give pause. Is my idol flirting with me?

Well, I can flirt back. "How old are you?"

He leans closer. "Old enough to know better. I shouldn't be sending gifts to someone so young, but I couldn't resist."

"It was nice of you." I bat my eyelashes at him, causing him to swallow hard.

As in I just made the great Intrepid react, sexually. My instructor in hand-to-hand combat told me being a girl was one of my greatest weapons, because I would be underestimated by my adversaries.

"I have to be honest with you," he says. "I bought it because—"

"You want me to introduce you to the twins?"

"Will they be at your party?"

"No."

"I'd still like to come."

"Why?"

He leans closer again. "Isn't it obvious?"

I slide under his arm and back away. "Actually, it's not."

"Fine. I'd like to meet the Prince."

"So go talk to him now."

He sighs like he's about to tell me a big secret. Like I wore him down, but I know better. One of his documented abilities was recruitment—his ability to get normal citizens to help him in the name of The Crown. I also read that his bullshit meter is high—that he can spot a lie from a mile away. I have to be totally on my game whenever he's around.

"I'm going to tell you the truth," he says. "I'm not here for the race. I work for the British government, and we're worried about the Prince's safety."

"So why don't you have your government call their government and set up a meeting?"

"Because his government isn't throwing your party."

"Do you think someone is going to try to kill the Prince at my party?"

"I don't know."

"Uh, huh. And exactly which part of the government do you work for?"

"MI6."

"A real-life James Bond, huh?" I laugh in his face. "You know, if you're trying to seduce me, you're working way too hard. The purse was a good start. You should have followed it up with a kiss, not some ridiculous story."

"I believe the Prince is in danger, and so are you."

"And how do I know he's not in danger from you?" I kiss his cheek. "Thanks for the bag."

Take that, Intrepid.

THE REST OF the evening continues with exquisite food and flowing drinks. The Prince and I take to the dance floor for a couple of hours until he asks if I'd like to go somewhere more private.

He takes my hand and leads me off the boat and toward the water, not back to his car like I expected.

"Where are you going?" Juan asks.

"I'd like to show the lovely Miss Von Allister the

gorgeous view of our great city at night."

"I don't think that's a good idea."

"I'm not asking for permission, Juan. This is a completely unplanned whim. Common sense tells us that anyone out to get me would have done so at the party. They couldn't scramble fast enough to plan anything right now. We'll be quick and perfectly safe."

He leads me to the end of the dock then turns me around to take in the view of Cap. The lights go up the hillside, showing off beautiful homes and a few sleek high-rises.

"It's gorgeous," I say, turning to face him.

He puts his lips on mine. "I think I'm falling for you, Huntley."

"You're standing next to the water at the end of a dock. One little push and you'd literally be falling," I tease, gently putting my hand against his chest and pretending to push.

He grabs my hand and flops backwards, taking us both into the water.

I take a deep breath just as we hit but still come up sputter-choking.

"You are totally insane! I love it. Even though you probably just ruined my dress."

"I'll buy you ten new ones." He pulls me close, kissing me.

"Your Royal Highness!" one of his bodyguards yells

as flashlights beam down on us.

He doesn't reply, just threads his hands through my hair and deepens our kiss with a dart of his tongue. The Prince is polite and well-mannered, asking for permission rather than assuming. It's sweet.

And fun to play along. Although, it's a little difficult to concentrate on kissing someone and feeling super sexy when your beaded cocktail dress suddenly feels like it weighs about two hundred thousand pounds, and even though you float in the salt water, you find yourself needing to tread water every so often so that you don't ruin your mission by drowning the Prince yourself, who is too busy caressing your back to worry about those pesky details.

It's also hard to kiss a prince who you are supposed to be protecting. Especially when you should have your eyes open to scan the area for danger—from assassins, sharks, whatever—and you're seriously considering using the knife blade in your shoe to cut yourself free of your dress.

I wiggle my toes. Shit. My shoes have drowned.

His hands move to cup my ass and give it a little squeeze.

I pull out of his embrace. "You know, it would be a pity if the newspapers reported tomorrow that our cause of death was that we were drowned by a beaded party dress."

He chuckles. "You, Lee, make me laugh."

"What did you just call me?" I ask as a memory flashes though my brain—fast and painful. But I have to ignore it.

"Lee, like short for Hunt-ley. I didn't think anyone probably called you Hunt. I'm sorry if that's too forward of me."

"You just had your tongue in my mouth and your hands on my ass, I'd say you've already been forward."

"And?"

"I like it. On both accounts."

He snaps his fingers, and two guards appear at the top of the dock. He helps the guards hoist all six hundred pounds of me out of the water.

The top of my silk chiffon dress has become transparent, allowing everyone in the vicinity—including two photographers who start snapping photos of me—to see my braless boobs, which are at attention from both the make-out session and the cool night air. The Prince's bodyguard graciously slips his jacket on me while the Prince comes up the ladder—which would have been my preference instead of looking like a damsel in distress being hoisted out.

"Prince Lorenzo! Prince Lorenzo, what happened?" the paparazzi yell.

"I got fresh, and Miss Von Allister threatened to push me in the water. Being the cad I am, I pulled her in with me."

I'm about to give a witty comeback when a red dot skitters across the Prince's head.

And I know what that means.

My heart races—adrenaline pumping through me.

I react immediately by leaping on top of him and knocking him to the deck just as a bullet hits one of the yachts behind us, quickly followed by the sound of a gun's retort.

The weapon is silenced but still makes a sound that you can't miss.

I know it won't take long for the shooter to align the next shot.

I grab the Prince around the waist and quickly roll us back off the dock and into the water. Based on the trajectory of the shot, the shooter is higher than us and that puts us at a big disadvantage.

Another shot hits the dock right where we were just lying and whizzes into the water.

I grab the Prince and pull him toward a boat, so we can use it as cover. Although a shot to one of the boat's fuel cells could cause us a lot of damage, I try not to think about that. Staying in the darkened water and with our heads low, I drag the Prince to safety.

The reporters scream. The Prince's guards yell for them to take cover while shouting orders to each other. They radio for backup and send men to search for the shooter.

But another shot rings out. This one hits the water where we rolled in, but is not close to where we are now.

I take a deep breath. I just saved the Prince.

Again.

What I need to do right now is capture the shooter and interrogate him, but it would probably look a tad suspicious if I took off running.

Maybe the guards will find and arrest him.

In the meantime, I need to keep the handsome man in front of me safe.

"We almost got shot," he states numbly.

"Yes, I think someone just tried to kill you again," I whisper. "Let's climb up onto this boat." I point at the ladder on a small yacht. The boat is dark and appears to be empty. I lost my clutch and shoes earlier. No way to get in touch with Ari for back up.

"You're shivering," the Prince says, wrapping his arms around me.

"So are you. It's the adrenaline rush. We're coming down. And we're wet."

He holds me close. "Did you just save my life again?"

"Maybe."

"How did you know?"

Before I can answer, twenty guards board the yacht, and I'm pulled away from the Prince.

"Stop it," he tells them. "Let her go."

"Your Highness, you narrowly escaped another assassination attempt."

"Only because *she* jumped on me."

"Don't you think that's a little convenient?"

"I'd say so, otherwise I'd be dead. No thanks to you lot."

"How did she know a shot was about to be fired, when your elite force did not?"

They all turn to me in question.

"There was a little red dot." I point to a spot on my own forehead.

"And you just happened to know that red light was from the scope of a sniper's rifle?"

"I like action movies. I just reacted." I shrug and try to look bewildered by it all.

The Prince marches through the guards and takes my face in his hands.

"Thank you." He shows his gratitude by giving me a sweet but epic kiss. Then he wraps an arm around me and turns to the guards. "You should be out looking for the shooter."

"We are, sir."

"Then get us home."

ONCE AT THE castle, and in the privacy of his bedroom, Lorenzo pulls me into a frantic kiss, then we strip each other out of our cold, wet clothes. We're naked and tightly pressed against each other, the heat warming us both.

It's clear that he wants to sleep with me.

And my body is responding in like.

He runs his mouth up the side of my neck and says, "I greatly desire you."

And I desire him, too. I'm attracted to him. Sleeping with him would be good for my mission. So what's stopping me?

I close my eyes and take a deep breath. "Lorenzo, I greatly desire you, as well, but I'm not sure this is a good idea."

"Why not?"

Why not is a good question. For the good of my mission, I should sleep with him. But I like him too much to do that. Which honestly, makes no sense. It's just that if I ever get to sleep with him, I want it to be me not the spy.

"Because we're all pumped up from surviving yet another attack together. I don't want that to interfere with how wonderful our courtship has been so far."

"Neither do I, but I think—"

We're interrupted by a knock on his door. "Prince Lorenzo," Juan says from the other side. "I'm afraid our national agency and military would like you to attend an emergency meeting. There is talk of calling off the race. Or putting you under house arrest until the threat passes."

"Do you know how long it will take?" he replies, still clutching me.

"Sorry, I do not."

Lorenzo reluctantly loosens our embrace. "Would you like to relax in my quarters until I'm finished? Although I regret that I have no idea when that will be."

"Would it be okay if I just went home? I wasn't home all day, and I'm supposed to meet with the caterers in the morning to finalize the brunch menu for race day. Although, I suppose we should consider cancelling that too."

"Don't be silly. We won't be cancelling either, and I *will be* attending both events. Get some sleep, my sweet, and I will call on you tomorrow. Juan will see you home."

He hands me a cashmere lounger to wear and quickly gets dressed in black slacks and a sweater. His hair is still damp, and he looks delicious, but we only have time for a quick goodbye kiss.

WHEN I GET home, I leave a note on Ellis's desk requesting a new phone.

On the way to my room, I stop to see if Ari is home, but he's not. I also discover that neither are Peter and Allie, which I guess isn't that big of a surprise as they mentioned that the yacht party would go on all night long. I guess I sort of thought the shots fired at the docks might have slowed it down, but no one probably heard it over the loud, pumping music.

I change out of Lorenzo's clothes, take a long hot shower, and grab a bottle of water out of the mini fridge in my suite. There's a document on my bedside table with a full write up on Intrepid who, contrary to popular belief, is not retired.

I sit at my desk, take some stationary out of the drawer, and write him a proper thank-you note for the evening bag and tuck in an invitation to brunch. I drop it off on Ellis's desk along with instructions to find out where William Gallagher is staying and to deliver it to him in the morning. Then I burn the documents about him in the fireplace.

When I get back to my room, I find Daniel lying across my bed wearing nothing but a pair of boxers.

"What are you doing here?"

"I don't have anywhere to stay. Thought I could stay with you," he replies, his blue eyes glittering.

"Embassy housing full?" I ask, sitting on the bed next to him.

"Actually, it is. I forgot to tell them I was coming back. Speaking of that, Lorenzo told me you slept with that British guy from the club."

"He passed out. We didn't have sex."

"You should have called me."

"You weren't in town yet. Who I should have called was Ellis, but it was very late and he'd been working hard on the impromptu pool party we decided to throw."

"It bothered me that you went home with him."

"Why?"

"It bothered the Prince, too."

"Why would it bother him?"

"He likes you."

"He's *liked* a lot of girls," I counter, rolling my eyes.

"He thinks you're different."

"Probably because I didn't fall into bed with him."

He grabs the front of his shirt that I'm wearing and slowly unbuttons it, holding my gaze. "Like you did with me?"

I give him a smirk. "And here I thought you took me home for pizza and video games."

"I took you home because you're beautiful," he says, sliding the shirt off my shoulder and kissing it. "I slept with you because you're fun to be around." His lips work their way up my neck until his face is right in front of mine. I get the dimple. "Plus, I couldn't let you continue to kick my ass at Battleground. I had to distract you."

"You weren't trying to distract me. I sat on your lap."

He nips at my lip then leans us back on the bed. "I liked that. So, have you banged the Prince yet?"

"If you and the Prince are so close, you should ask him yourself."

"I'm asking you," he says, trailing his hand up my thigh.

"It's none of your business, but if you must know, he has more old-fashioned values."

"Bullshit, he's screwed more women than . . . *Oh.*" Daniel's hand stops moving and he exhales deeply, almost like he just got punched in the gut.

"Oh, what?"

"He actually likes you."

"Maybe," I say.

"He might be a prince, but I rocked your world." He's right. He did, but I think that's all it is for him. Just sex.

"You rocked my world?" I tease. "What, is this the 90s?"

His hand moves further up, his finger twisting around the lace of my thong, as he kisses me. "You know we're good together."

"I bet you say that to all the girls."

He stops kissing me to pull a tabloid off the nightstand and shove it in my face. "I picked this up at the airport. They're already talking engagement."

"That's because Ophelia and Viktor got engaged at the—"

"No, they're talking about *your* future engagement."

"Do you care what they say?"

"Depends if it's true."

"Daniel," I sigh.

"What?"

I can't believe I'm going to say this. I don't want to say this. But I have to. For the good of my mission. And for my own good. "You're welcome to stay here at the villa, just not in my room."

He nods but doesn't move. I sit up, buttoning the shirt.

He cups my cheek in his hand. "Are you in love with Lorenzo?"

"I care for him."

"And do you care for me?"

I gulp, even though I was trained not to give away my feelings through nonverbal communication. Lying is second nature for me. I'm good at it. But I can't seem to lie to him. Not about this.

I look down and simply nod. Because I do care about him, even though I shouldn't.

"Then I'll stay in the room next door," he says, getting out of bed and picking up his clothes. "I want to be close by. I heard about the attempts on his life and fear you may be in danger by association. It was way too easy for me to sneak into your room."

"I really don't want you to leave," I admit.

"I can just sleep in here, if you want. We don't have to, you know. I just want to keep you safe."

Which is as soothing as it is ironic.

MISSION: DAY SEVEN

Two men are alone in a large, ornate library having a terse discussion.

"The papers say she's going to be the next Princess of Montrovia. She may be doing part of her mission a little too well."

"She's saved him from three separate assassination attempts. I'd say that's pretty damn good for a brand new agent."

"Yes, but is she making any progress on the case?" the leader of Black X asks.

The former Dean of Blackwood Academy frowns but does not reply.

"I'd hate to see all her training go to waste because she decides she'd rather be royal. Maybe we need to dangle a carrot in front of her."

"I think you're playing with fire."

"Do what you need to do, old man."

"Do you have no conscience? Have you ever stopped to think about what effect this could have on her? She's just a girl."

"She's soon to be nineteen and has always been very mature for her age. Remind me again why she wants to work for Black X?"

"To avenge her parents' deaths," the Dean says with a sigh, knowing he won't win this battle.

"Then our goals are in alignment. We will both do whatever it takes—no matter the price. The world as we know it may depend on our commitment. Make the call."

THE FORMER DEAN goes into his office at Black X headquarters and calls the villa in Montrovia on a secure line.

"Hello?" she says, her voice sounding different than he is used to. He realizes why. She sounds happy. She's in her element.

"Word on the street is you will become a princess. Is that what you want?"

"That's what every girl wants, apparently," she fires back.

"But you're not every girl."

"No, I'm not. And you know what I want."

"To be a member of Black X?"

"And to find the man who killed my parents."

"If you succeed in this mission, they will help you."
He hates lying to her. The man who killed her mother is
dead. Double-crossed by the man who hired the hit on
her mother, if rumors are correct. Hopefully he will be
spared from having to tell her that truth.

"I've saved him three times already."

"Protecting him is only part of your mission. Keep
that in mind."

"Sir, do you think I'm doing well?"

"That remains to be seen."

"I found out about the watch you gave—"

He hangs up before she can say another word and
prays the line was indeed secure.

MY CALL WITH the Dean gets disconnected, and he
doesn't call back, so I return to my room from the
terrace, where I took the call.

Daniel is still asleep, so I slip back into bed. He pulls
me into his chest, wraps his arms around me, and makes
a cute little mumbled sound as his lips land on my
shoulder.

I take a few moments to bask in the glow of being in
his arms.

I realize now it was a mistake to let him sleep with
me last night. Our just sleeping together felt more

intimate than if we would have had sex. I can't get attached to him. No matter how hot or tender he may be.

He's not my mission.

And I need to forget about him.

While he was off in Switzerland, I pushed him out of my mind and focused on the Prince. And I've been successful in my mission of protecting him. But the Dean is right. I've been spending too much time doing that and not enough time tracking down who is responsible. But it's really hard to do both.

Today the drivers qualify for their positions in the race, and I feel like I need to do the same—move fast, figure out who is behind the plot, and take the checkered flag.

The streets will be packed. There have been events all week, but today kicks off a forty-eight hour continuous party that ends in grand form with the winning driver and his team being honored at the Queen's Ball.

Which means the clock is ticking, and I'm quickly running out of time.

I reluctantly leave Daniel, throw on some yoga clothes, and then go to Ari's room.

"Morning," he says. "I was just coming to get you." He leads me to the garage and then down the secret elevator so we can talk privately. I look around at the space. I must have been too overwhelmed my first time here to notice everything. It's literally like a secret lair. It makes me feel like a real spy, and I can see that Ari has been spending some free time down here, based on a large whiteboard covered with notes in a scratchy print.

"Okay, so let's walk through this. We know the threat: Kill the Prince. We know why: Control the Strait. We know how: Storming the castle. Attempted poisoning. Attempted shooting. What we don't know is who is behind the attempts or what they will try next."

"Okay."

"So the who. Obvious answers are who is next in line. Ophelia. Then Clarice. I think it's safe to add Viktor to the list based on the fact that he and Ophelia were together and the fact that they started dating days before her father was killed. Then we have the random factor, some sort of terror group. What do you think of my assumptions so far?"

"If you consider the Queen's Ball is where all the royals on the succession list will be gathered, then I think you have to consider a bombing plot, where they would just blow up the place. If you consider the castle breech a warm-up, then I'd be concerned about them sending in a small, highly-trained Special Forces team to take them out. Think about it. You will even have the heads of the military at the Queen's Ball."

"I wonder if any of the heirs aren't planning on being there."

"We should try to find out, although if it was my plot, I'd say I was coming and *take ill* the night of."

"Meaning whoever doesn't show up, could be behind the plot."

"I suppose, but I feel like that's widening the net too much. We need to focus on our top suspects."

"Agreed," Ari says. "So, I'd say we have our top scenarios. I should also add that I spent the night at the cousins' mansion."

"Did you and Clarice get freaky?"

"No. I pretended to be drunk, so they put me to bed. Once everyone went to sleep, I had a look around."

"Did you find anything?"

"There was something interesting that I *didn't* find."

"What didn't you find?" I ask.

"Not one single photo of their father in the entire place."

"Because it's too painful?"

"I think they didn't really like him much. And based off a snide comment Ophelia made regarding Prince Lorenzo, I'm thinking they don't like him either."

"Because they didn't get to grow up like he did? Do they resent him?"

"It sounds like it. I also found this." Ari connects his phone to a cable and a photo shoots onto the screen.

"What's that? It looks like someone built a modern city on top of one of those alien crop circles."

"*This* was in Clarice's study and is a plan for the Terra Project."

"She couldn't have come up with that herself. Did she?"

"No, it's the work of an American scientist." He flashes another picture. A map of Montrovia with the crop circles drawn over the top of the casino.

"I don't see any of the pretty yachts," I mention.

"Yeah, me either."

"But the castle is unaffected."

"Strange, isn't it? Does Miss Save The World want to move into it? Control her country?"

"Her little project with everyone working for the greater good sounds a lot like socialism," I admit. "Could she have twisted her hate for her father into a hate for the whole country?"

"That's what I'm wondering. Last night, she spent a lot of time speaking to the Saudi Prince."

"Lorenzo met with him twice. He's supposedly concerned for their oil shipments. Why would she be telling him about the project?"

"Maybe if she succeeds, she will need help overthrowing the military," he suggests.

"But then they would be in control, not her."

"What if she sold the rights to the Strait of Montrovia, but was allowed to keep her country in exchange for military protection?"

"Holy shit, Ari."

"My thoughts exactly."

"So you think she had someone kill her father and make it look like a suicide, now she's trying to get rid of Lorenzo, and then she'll have her own sister killed?"

"I suspect so. What do you think?"

"Do we have any further information on the men who committed the first two assassination attempts?"

He shuffles through a pile of papers. "Yes. The dots have been connected. All three belong to a radical environmental group participating in eco-terrorism. They use violence in an attempt to protect the environment. It's odd, though. Although, they use violence to disrupt corporations whose environmental policies they disagree with, they rarely kill."

"So, did she hire them or is this bigger than her? Could she just be a pawn in this game?"

"I'm not sure." He pulls up the Terra Project's website. I watch words flash across the screen.

Imagine a world with no politics. No poverty. No debt. No suffering. A world where everyone is equal. Every citizen would have their basic needs met. Water, food, shelter, transportation. Where we use clean energies like solar, water, and wind power and stop depleting our natural resources. We would raise the standard of living for the entire world. Imagine what we could achieve together.

"My plan is to stick to her like glue for the next two

days," Ari states. "Your job is to make sure the Prince stays safe."

"My head is spinning, Ari." Particularly because I must complete the rest of my mission: Eliminate the threat. Clarice would be easy to take out. I could order brunch, go kill her, and be back before it was served. But I need to be certain she's the threat before I do.

"I've been thinking about it for a few hours," Ari says. "We're on the right track."

"Do you ever get scared?" I ask him.

"Yeah," he says, wrapping his arm around my neck and giving me a stiff hug. "But we'll get through it together."

THE PRINCE CALLS and says he's going to be in meetings most of the day and will hopefully meet up with us later.

Daniel, Ari, Peter, Allie, and I decide to go watch some of the qualifying.

I was worried about how I was going to juggle Daniel and the Prince, but it's easy since only one of them is here, but I know it won't last long. After all I'd read about Daniel, I thought I could sleep with him, he'd lose interest, and move on to his next conquest. But he hasn't. I suggested rather than doing the whole yacht-Amber Room VIP version of watching qualifying that we do what normal people do and sit on the hill leading up to the castle on blankets and take a picnic.

As we're looking for a place to sit, Peter asks, "What's with all the military?"

"A big event like this," Daniel says, "they have to be vigilant. And I would think it helps the people feel safe. Especially after the attacks on the Prince."

"Feel safe or be safe?" Ari ponders, spreading out a blanket and plopping our gourmet picnic basket down.

"That is the question," Peter replies. "However, Montrovia is such a unique country in that it has no poverty. Those who want to do business within Montrovia have very strict guidelines regarding wages. From the janitor and maids, to the gardeners—all are paid handsomely. Have you ever been to a coastal town and the closer you get to the beach, the higher the cost of fuel and food?"

"Yes," we all say.

"That's not allowed here. No price gouging. Food and wine is cheap, and all citizens are covered by their top-notch medical insurance and facilities. They are a peaceful sovereign state and don't stick their noses in world affairs. They have a capable army, elite forces to guard their borders, and a world-class maritime division which controls the Strait of Montrovia. For many centuries, there has been only peace."

"Sounds like Montrovia has it all figured out," I reply, wondering why Peter is so knowledgeable on this.

"Although they allow visitors to come spend their

money, they have very strict immigration policies and visas. Citizenship is what you are born into. It's the only way to make a small country work, probably. The average United States citizen can't afford to get sick. Here, they focus on taking care of their own."

"Enough talk of politics," Daniel says to them. "We need to open the champagne and see what goodies your chef packed."

LATER, I WANDER away from the group, checking out the crowd of people on the hill and noticing that I have a very good view of the Royal Yacht, where the Prince and I will be watching the race tomorrow. How easy would it be to hide a rifle in a picnic basket, screw it together, and take a shot? Or worse, launch a rocket-propelled grenade. We'd be gone in an instant.

And I can't die yet.

Not until I avenge my mother's death.

After that, I don't care much about living.

"Hey, where have you been?" Daniel says, wandering up to me. "I've been looking for you."

"I snuck out for a smoke?" I lie.

"You don't smoke," he says, smacking my ass and causing me to jump. I tumble forward, almost falling to the ground, but Daniel's strong arm reaches out and grabs me.

"You and those heels," he says, causing an instant

flashback to me in his townhouse wearing nothing but.

AFTER A LONG day in the sun, we head back home. Daniel wants to play video games, but Ari beats me to it, the two of them quickly engaging in some fake battle together.

I'm lying across a chaise watching them when my phone buzzes. I walk out on one of the villa's sweeping terraces to take the call.

"You have the tabloids all in a tizzy now," the Prince says.

"Why's that?"

"Your picnic today with Daniel."

"I had a picnic with Allie, Peter, my brother, *and* Daniel, as well as some of Peter's friends who showed up."

"It's quiet where you are," he says. "Are you not partying at the Amber Room?"

"No, Peter and Allie went, but Ari is still hung over from last night, I think, and Daniel is exhausted from his photo shoot with the Swiss bikini team, so they are on the couch playing video games."

"Have you slept with Daniel?" he asks bluntly.

I hesitate, wondering if I should tell him the truth. Last time he asked, I simply said no comment. This could be a deal breaker.

I end up going with part of the truth.

"Yes. I slept with him the night we met. I honestly never expected to see him again."

"But you haven't slept with me?"

"Sleeping with you feels like more of a commitment. I like you. Daniel and I flirted and fell into bed. You have done that many times, I'm told, so you should know the difference between a thoughtless fling and something that feels more—important."

"So you fancy me?"

"I think I do. Where are you? It's quiet there."

"In my chamber. I've had a full day of meetings."

"Would you like some company?"

"Depends who would be coming."

"Just me."

"Will you spend the night with me tonight?"

"If you would like me to."

"I would very much like you to."

"What shall I wear?"

"Preferably nothing. Have you had dinner?"

"Not really."

"Then we shall dine in my suite."

"So I shouldn't show up naked?"

He laughs. "It would save the guards from having to search you for weapons."

"Lorenzo."

"What, Lee?"

"I'm really glad you called."

I'M PULLING MY car out of the garage when William Gallagher jumps out of the bushes by the gate and into my passenger seat.

"What are you doing?"

"Going for a ride with you. Where are you going? You look nice by the way."

"Thank you. And not that it's any of your business, but I'm going to the palace."

"I really do work for the British government. We believe another attempt on the Prince's life is imminent. He should cancel the Queen's Ball."

"He won't. He said the Ball is bigger than one man."

"You need to get him to change his mind."

When I stop at the light, he gets out of the car and slips into the night.

THE PRINCE AND I have a lovely dinner, then he challenges me to a game of chess, so we sit across from each other at a table in his private study and start the match.

After a few moves, I take one of his pawns.

"Merda," he says, taking off his shirt and throwing it over to the couch.

"You have a scrumptious chest, so I'm not complaining, but why did you just take your shirt off? Are you hot?"

"Did I forget to mention that we're playing strip

chess?"

"I didn't know there was such a thing."

"Well, if there wasn't, there is now." He uses his rook to take my knight and then raises an eyebrow and smirks at me. All I have on is a dress and a pair of heels. I will be stripped in no time.

"Do you want to sleep with me?" I ask him, rather than removing my dress.

"I very much do."

"And do you envision this as how our first time happens? Stripping because of a chess game?" I bite my lower lip. I'm really nervous that he's going to tell me to leave. That he's sick of waiting—something he's not used to.

"I'm not sure," he says tentatively.

"Lorenzo, there's nothing I'd like more than to shove all these chess pieces off the board and have you do me right here on the table, but—" I run my hand through my hair. I'm struggling with this in a way that has nothing to do with my mission. My feelings for him have crossed the line, so I go with it and tell him the truth. "It's odd, really. I'm not at all against casual sex. I like it very much, and it's something I enjoy participating in. It's almost a sport in my mind. A game. But you—I don't want you to be a game." I look down. "If you want me to leave now, I understand."

He grasps my hand. "I don't want you to leave, Huntley."

I look up into his eyes—eyes filled with love and caring that words have yet to confess—and know I'll never be the kind of ruthless spy I'm supposed to be.

MISSION: DAY EIGHT

OUR VILLA IS crowded with people we met this week, and everyone is excited for the race today. Allie is in her element, acting as a hostess, which I appreciate. She's really a sweet girl, and I can't help but wish that we could stay friends.

She and Peter join the Prince and me at a table, and Peter tells us about the work he's going to be doing for his father.

"One of the things our company does is go into war-torn areas and help the government rebuild. In the desert where sand, sun, and wind are plentiful, building concrete homes and harnessing sun and wind power is not only green, but cheap and efficient."

"So, how are you going to help with that?" I ask.

"They built a few test towns years ago. We're going

back in to study their effectiveness."

"That sounds interesting," Allie says, even though she looks bored.

"It is," he agrees and continues talking. I mimic Allie's look of boredom, but I'm not at all. I hadn't realized that his father was involved in something like this. "We could build pod cities like these all over the world. Turning it into a global environmental initiative."

"It sounds like the Terra Project that Clarice was talking about the other night," I mention casually.

He rolls his eyes. "*Obviously*, that's where Clarice and I would disagree. This is a commercial project for us. We don't agree with the whole *bartering* deal. We're in this to make money. To sell our cities to the governments of the world."

"I like the idea of my country leaving a smaller environmental footprint, but I can't imagine my capital city any way other than how it is now," Lorenzo states, causing me to shake my head in agreement.

"Cap is beautiful," I add.

"Honestly," Peter says, "the whole thing seems stupid to me, too. We already have amazing cities in the world. It's not like anyone is going to tear them down and rebuild. But my dad said I have to go if I want a cushy job, so it is what it is. I heard they don't allow alcohol in the country he's sending me to, so I'm not planning to stay long. If you ask me, that's why they are so jumpy over there."

"Because some religions don't believe in the consumption of alcohol?" I ask incredulously. Peter is a
stupid, pompous ass who hasn't got a clue about the real
world. Although, I doubt he would care to know.

"Lizzie, I didn't know you would be here today," the
Prince says, suddenly looking up and looking nervous.
I'm wondering if she's some stalker girl he's been
sleeping with when he turns to me. "Huntley, I'd like to
introduce you to Lady Elizabeth Palomar. She and I are
old friends."

"I've known him since we were mere babes," Elizabeth says, shaking my hand. "I heard he was here. I hope
it's okay that I came to your party."

"It's lovely to meet you," I say sincerely, but I'm
wondering why she is here and if she's a threat. "I'm glad
you could join us."

"It's my pleasure."

"Did you come back in town just for the race?" the
Prince asks her.

"Of course. If I missed the Queen's Ball, my mother
would probably disown me."

"Where are you living?" Allie asks.

"She's studying art in Paris," the Prince answers for
her.

Lizzy smiles at him in a way that makes me wonder
about their past. There's an undercurrent of flirtation

going on, and I'm not sure I like it, or her.

THE HARBOR, THE grandstands, the hills, and the streets are full of people cheering for the race.

We're on the Prince's boat, and that alone is a logistical nightmare for his security. There are men on wave runners guarding the yacht's perimeter. There are men controlling access to the boat from the docks, and while they are not allowing anyone on the boat who wasn't invited, there are boatloads of partiers anchored on both sides of us. Race-goers are screened for weapons before they enter the area, and the local police and National Guard are out in full force.

Like the Queen's Garden Party, I worry about threats from the air. There are two blimps and numerous helicopters circling the track. The hill to the castle is straight across from us. Most of it is open with people sitting on blankets having picnics, but there is an area at the top full of trees. I wonder if that area is being patrolled. It's where I'd go if I was trying to take out the Prince.

Lady Elizabeth and Allie have become fast friends. They walk to the railing where I'm standing and hand me a flute of champagne.

"You looked stressed," Allie says.

"I'm fine. It's just there are so many people here, and I'm worried about Lorenzo's safety. There was talk of calling off the Queen's Ball."

"Speaking of the Ball," Allie gushes. "What are your dresses like? Mine is a pale yellow Dior."

"That will look wonderful on you," Elizabeth says. "Mine is a floral, off the shoulder Pierre Galante. He's a local designer. What about you, Huntley?"

"Uh, my dress is red."

"Bold choice," Elizabeth says. "Usually red is the color the Queen, herself, wears."

My eyes widen. "Does that mean no one else is supposed to wear that color? Lorenzo bought the dress. It was the one that ended the fashion show, remember that one, Allie?"

Allie claps her hands. "Of course, I remember! It was to die for!"

"But if he knows that's the color his mother always wears, why would he do that?"

"Maybe it's intentional," Elizabeth says. "I keep reading about the two of you. You've had a whirlwind romance from the sounds of it."

"It's really kind of crazy that people could speculate the future of our relationship when we've known each other for a short time."

"He isn't called the Playboy Prince for nothing, Huntley," Elizabeth says, resting her hand gently on my forearm. "During Race Week, his behavior is usually particularly scandalous. This year, it is not. Because of you. I'm glad he's finally found someone who's intelligent and sweet." She lowers her voice. "And not a money grubbing hoebag."

I quickly change my mind about liking Elizabeth.

I'M DRESSED AND ready for the ball in a red gown that literally makes me feel like a princess. My hair is done in a pretty updo that sweeps back into a sleek, twisted knot with some complicated braiding holding back my bangs.

"Are you ready?" I call out, before I open the French doors to the Prince's study. I've been getting ready for hours. He probably showered, shaved, and dressed in fifteen minutes.

"I am," he replies, as I fling them open.

He stands up from behind his desk, looking more handsome than ever with his hair slicked back and wearing the navy dress uniform of the Montrovian maritime forces. It has elaborate heavy gold braiding, thick red trim, and numerous royal and military medallions. When I'm hanging out with him, it's sort of easy to forget that he's a prince, but there's no mistaking it tonight.

"You look stunning," he says, crossing the space between us and holding out his hand. I place my hand in his, and he spins me around in a dance move, then dips and kisses me.

"You look amazing, too. I've never seen you all

decked out like this. You actually look like a real prince."

This gets a chuckle out of him. "I have a surprise for you," he says, leading me back to his desk and pointing to a box.

I open it to find a pair of heels nestled in tissue. "They look like glass slippers!"

"They are Swarovski crystals cut to look like diamonds set on a base more comfortable for dancing in than glass."

"I've never seen anything like this. And I have done a fair amount of shopping in this city."

"They were made just for you."

I kiss him.

"They're beautiful. Thank you so much." I slip off the gorgeous, glitter-covered designer heels I had on, that now pale in comparison.

When I sit down to put them on, he says, "Let me," and slides them on my feet.

I stand up and spin. "I think now I'm really ready!"

"Not quite yet," he says, leading me through the palace to a vault where a guard opens it and joins us inside. "Pick something to wear tonight."

Around me is so much sparkle I can barely think straight. Diamonds may be my kryptonite.

"Oh, I couldn't."

"Then I will choose for you." He studies my dress, runs a finger across my cleavage, and kisses my neck. It's hard not to fall completely under his spell.

"This one," he says, selecting an elegant diamond and ruby teardrop choker with matching bracelet and placing them on me. "Now, you are fit to be my date," he teases.

I run my hands under his jacket. "I think tonight, after the ball, I'd like to, uh, play *chess* again."

He smiles, knowing I'm not really referring to the game, but rather consummating our relationship.

"I am up for that challenge," he says, taking my hand in his and kissing it. "Let's go make our grand entrance."

THE BALL IS a whirlwind of introductions and dancing. The Prince is a good dancer who leads me around the dance floor in a way that makes me feel incredibly light on my feet—or, maybe it's the shoes.

I also never knew the waltz could be so utterly romantic.

Partway through the evening, I excuse myself to freshen up and find Daniel waiting for me when I come out of the ladies room.

"You need to dance with me," he demands.

"I can't. I'm the Prince's date. People will talk."

"It's not like you're married," he argues.

"No, but people act like we should be. Which is crazy. I just met him this week."

"You met me eight days ago. And you're wearing red

again. It's driving me nuts. Have you slept with him?"

"My answer to that question is the same as it's been the other times you have asked. It's none of your business."

"You went to his place late last night."

"And when I came back home, you were passed out on the couch. I haven't had sex with him. Yet."

"Thus the jewels," Daniel says, rolling his eyes. "He's working hard to get you into bed."

"Or maybe I'm just lucky."

He holds my gaze for a beat. "Actually, Huntley, you haven't gotten lucky yet tonight." He pushes me back into the bathroom and locks the door behind us.

"I thought you and the Prince were friends?"

"We're not that good of friends. Besides, the life of a princess would bore you."

"Every girl dreams of becoming a princess. Why wouldn't I like it?"

"Because I'm not the Prince."

I laugh.

And that's when he kisses me. It's possessive, passionate, and full of heat.

Body language and nonverbal clues are important in espionage. The body often can't lie the way the tongue can. But even though Daniel is kissing me hotly, his body language is tentative. His hands are motionless at his sides. He isn't sure how I will react, so he isn't all in.

No one likes to be rejected, especially someone with an ego like his.

I slip my fingers into his dark hair and let my body do the talking, even though I know I shouldn't.

Which is what he was waiting for. He pushes me against the wall, delving his tongue deeply into my mouth while he's shoving up the layers of my gown.

My body is on fire with desire, and Daniel is ready to fulfill my need. His need. Our need.

But then a vision of the Prince getting killed while I'm in the bathroom with the Vice President's son flashes in my head.

I reluctantly rip my lips away. "Daniel, wait. I can't."

He doesn't say a word, just angrily walks out the door—leaving me breathless and unfulfilled.

I TAKE A few moments to compose myself. Fix my lipstick. Check my hair. Anything not to think about why I stopped him. Because the answer scares me.

When I meet the Prince at our dinner table, he says, "I saw Daniel follow you toward the ladies' room. When he came back a few minutes ago, he seemed upset. Did you two have a row?"

"No, it's just that he wants, um—"

"You? Again?" the Prince asks, bluntly.

"Possibly. I'm sorry." I let out a big sigh.

The Prince takes my hand in his and kisses it. "No

need to be sorry, my dear. You have the ability to put a man under your spell."

"Except that I gave *you* my love potion."

His face beams—apparently that was the answer he needed to hear—as he takes me into his arms and leads me out to the dance floor.

I can't help but get a little swept away by the grandeur of it all. The ornate ballroom. The live orchestra. The waltzing. The gowns. The jewels. When I was waiting in the Prince's residence the other day, I saw a tabloid that mentioned my parents were killed when I was young. The headline said that the orphan was dating the Prince, like we are part of some fairytale.

I don't care much about what the papers say—I consider it mindless babble—but that headline struck me.

I never thought of myself as an orphan. My parents died, and I went to live at Blackwood.

The other night when Daniel slept in my bed, I confessed that the label bothered me.

He hugged me. Held me. Kissed the top of my head. And even though I knew I should have kicked his muscular body out of my bed, I couldn't.

I know he's mad at me now. I shouldn't have allowed myself to lose control like that for even a second. I am on a mission.

I am on a mission.

And I have to succeed.

THE BALL IS over, the guests have left, and I'm extremely relieved we managed to get through it without another assassination attempt. The Prince has invited a few of us to stay, the guys planning to smoke cigars on this clear, starry night. The breeze is chilly, so a steward lights a fire in a built-in pit, then takes our drink order.

We all huddle around the fire for warmth, the boys passing around a lighter to start their cigars.

Allie asks me to run to the restroom with her. She's quite tipsy and would probably get lost, so I agree to take her.

The Prince gives me a sweet kiss, and mutters something about missing me while I'm gone. Daniel watches the Prince's show of affection with a scowl. Ari and Peter are too busy trying to light their cigars to notice we're leaving.

I help Allie into the castle and down the hall. It's taking a while because she's drunker than I thought and keeps running into the wall. She giggles and says something about it jumping out in front of her.

I finally grab her elbow and lead her.

We're a few steps from the entrance to the bathroom when she pukes all over her ball gown and the polished marble floor. Then she lays down in it and starts crying.

I haven't drunk more than a glass of champagne all

night, but the smell makes me sick. I summon a guard, who summons a steward, who summons a janitor.

I hear cheers from the guys outside, their cigars probably finally lit. I wish I was out there enjoying myself.

I move Allie into the bathroom, leaning her against the wall near the toilet, where she gets sick again.

I pat her arm. "I'm going to get Peter so he can take you home. You stay right here."

"Peter doesn't love me like he should. I want you to bring Ari," she says with a sob.

Honestly, I doubt she wants either boy to see her like this, but I just nod in agreement.

I go back down the hall, noticing the sound of my heels clicking on the marble.

The guys must have quieted down.

Which is odd.

I step outside and have to blink to believe what I'm seeing. The boys aren't smoking cigars.

They aren't standing around the fire anymore. No one is.

My skin prickles.

I hadn't heard a thing.

No guns, no fighting, no shouting.

Where could they have gone?

But then I see two bodies twisted on the ground. At the far side of the courtyard, several men are bundling what looks like two more bodies into a van.

Lorenzo is my first thought. I take off at a sprint as the van pulls away. There's no way I can catch it.

I head for the bodies.

Daniel is one of them.

He's lying prone, one arm under his body, the other stretched out beside him. He's not moving. Not at all. My heart breaks into pieces, thinking he's dead. Thinking that I've failed him. That I've failed them all.

I roll him over, bracing to find blood. There is none. His clothes are intact. His head flops to one side, his eyes closed.

Tears form in my eyes as my fingers dance frantically across his neck, trying to find a pulse. I give a sigh of relief when I feel the regular thump-thump of his heart beating.

Then I see something on the side of Daniel's neck.

It's a tranquilizer dart. That's how they got all four of them so silently and so fast.

Peter is the other body on the ground. He has a pulse, too. Whatever they've been shot with is just a sedative. They weren't meant to die. But who knows what's happened to Ari and the Prince.

I roll Peter and Daniel onto their sides, neither one moving.

I give my fingers a kiss, press it against Daniel's forehead, and whisper, *I love you.*

I take a deep breath, trying to let go of my emotions

and focus on what drives me.

But I find it to be the same answer. *Love.* I've come to care for both the Prince and Daniel, not to mention Ari.

This is my mission. My love. My pain. My past. All muddled together, like a song inside my soul.

I stand quickly and spring to action. I use my phone to call the emergency number, recite my access code, and calmly tell the voice on the other end to alert the Montrovian guard that the Prince has been kidnapped. I hear a wild babbling chatter, but I hang up, knowing they'll figure it out.

I look down at my heels. My wrist. Instead of my father's watch, I'm wearing a diamond and ruby bracelet. Instead of my teched-out heels, I'm wearing the ones the Prince gave me.

I have no car.

No gun.

Only the phone in my hand.

And me.

I take off running, hoping it will be enough.

I DITCH THE heels and chase after the van, but it had a head start. I cut through the rose garden and see tail lights disappearing around the bend. I race past the guards, yelling that the Prince has been kidnapped. I leave them, radioing frantic messages as I push on, heading north, in the direction of the van.

I leave the grounds by scaling the castle wall, jumping over it, then running as fast as I can down the hill we sat on to watch qualifying. Where all the guards are, I have no idea.

I race into the town center, passing lines of luxurious storefronts. My lungs are burning, but I don't slow my pace.

I have to keep going.

But the tail lights have gone. The van has gone.

The Prince has . . . I take a deep breath. I'm not ready to admit that yet. I can't fail.

I have to find them.

A Jaguar approaches, heading in the opposite direction. The engine rumbles. It slows, the headlights blinding me. The engine growls, tires squeal, and the Jag rotates in the street, swirling around. The headlights are no longer blinding. The car slides to the curb next to me. The driver leans over and flips open the passenger door. I stumble to a halt.

"Get in," a British voice says.

It's Gallagher! I could kiss him, only I don't. I sink into the passenger seat just as my lungs are about to give out.

"Someone just kidnapped the Prince," I sputter, "and my brother." I point down the street. "Go!"

He floors it, causing the engine to crackle and roar.

I'm shoved back into the seat as we race down the street.

"A black van," I say. "They got onto the castle grounds somehow. I think they shot them all with tranquilizer darts. They left Daniel Spear and Peter Prescott, took Lorenzo and Ari."

"A black van?" he says. "That should make things easy. In the dark. At night."

I sigh. "Just keep going."

He does, weaving the Jag between traffic and junctions, hurtling through lights at the last moments of yellow. He's hunched forward. Staring. But he's right. Finding a black van in the dark, isn't going to be easy.

"Wait," I say.

He slows a fraction, and looks over at me.

"Ari puts trackers on people." I wave my phone. "I have an app."

"Why would he *need* to track people?"

"Oh, he doesn't," I lie. "He's, um, really smart and trying to create the next great technology."

"I see," Gallagher says, totally unconvinced.

"And since you asked for my help, I guess, technically, I'm a British spy like you. And I think it's up to us to save them."

"I've created a monster," Gallagher says, rolling his eyes at her, but at the same time pressing down on the accelerator. "Just tell me where to go."

"I don't know for sure, but keep going north, that's

the direction they were headed."

I open the app Terrance installed on both my and Ari's phones, praying Ari actually did put a tracker on Clarice, and hopefully himself or the Prince. There are colored dots sprinkled on a map. The dots don't have names. Two of the dots are literally on top of each other in the location of the Prince's cousins' mansion. Must be Viktor and Ophelia going at it. They did sneak out of the ball early.

There's a single dot in a separate part of the house, but that doesn't make sense. Why would someone kidnap them and take them there?

I widen the map's scope and find more dots. One appears to be circling the other.

"Here," I shout over the engine's roar. "This has to be them."

I point to a right turn. Gallagher squeals the tires, barely making the corner, then we scream off toward the docks, and hopefully to Ari and the Prince.

THE FOG LIFTS from Ari's mind. Small flashes of consciousness. Lights and sounds. He can't move. The tightness of ropes is cutting across his arms, chest, and ankles.

The light is dim. His head sways uncontrollably. He sees benches and machines. He's in a warehouse, and by the look of it, an unused one.

The Prince is tied to a chair beside him, his head is slumped forward. Behind him, there is movement. He feels a blow across the back of his head. His balance swims, and he screws his eyes shut.

"The tranquilizers are wearing off," a voice says. A female voice.

Ari forces his eyes back open. There are men in military fatigues patrolling the room, watching from windows.

A woman has her back to Ari. She checks her watch. "Is the boat ready?"

It's the same woman's voice. A nagging memory swirls in his foggy mind.

"Ready for departure," says one of the men.

The woman stands in front of Ari for a minute. He keeps his head low, avoiding eye contact, trying to get his brain to work. To figure out what happened. But then he remembers the sting in his neck. The realization that he was shot with something. He shakes the grogginess from his head while he tries to assess his situation.

The woman turns around and swings her arm at Ari, slapping him across the face. He jerks his head up, his eyes wide.

"You were snooping around my house," she yells. "What did you see?"

Ari shakes his head. "I don't know what you are talking about. Why do you have us tied up?"

She leans closer to him. "You're lying. I'm going to ask one more time before I kill you. And if you don't give me the right answer, I'm going to kill your airhead sister just for fun. What. Did. You. See?"

The Prince lifts his head. Ari can see him fighting against the drug in his system. The Prince rocks from side to side, trying to figure out why he can't move, then the realization.

He sees his cousin yelling at Ari and says, "What's going on? Why are we tied up? Why are you threatening him?"

His cousin moves to stand in front of him and gives his face a slap. "You, my cousin, are about to be put on a boat and taken out to sea, never to be seen again. Then *I* will rule Montrovia."

She grabs two handkerchiefs and shoves them in their mouths, so no one will hear them scream when they are fed to the sharks.

SPY GIRL IS directing Gallagher through the industrial area surrounding the docks.

"Does anyone ever call you Bill?" she asks.

"No," he replies.

"How about Will?"

"No."

"No nicknames? Nothing anyone calls you?"

"Nope."

"Weird," she says, but she's disappointed. She wishes he would have told her the truth about who he is. She looks back down at her phone. "Oh, wait! Turn right, right here! Then a quick left. Okay, now stop."

He draws the Jaguar up to a quiet halt and puts the car in park.

"I'll walk the rest of the way," she says.

"*You* are not going anywhere. It's much too dangerous. Stay in the car."

She doesn't have time to persuade or argue. This is her mission, and she has no idea which side he's really on. When the man known as Intrepid looks around, sizing up the area, she gets ready. When he looks back at her, she throws her arm out, violently driving the heel of her palm to his jaw. His head snaps back, bouncing off the headrest, and he slumps forward. Out.

"Sorry," she says quietly as she jumps out of the car and tears down the street, checking the location app and slowing as she gets closer. She stays in the shadows to analyze her surroundings.

Old warehouse by the water.

Two men guarding the perimeter. No automatic weapons. Each armed with a pistol.

The roof is tinged with moonlight. She sees no sign of activity.

No snipers on the roof.

Dim light filters from a window. It flickers as figures

pass by. Once. Twice.

Two more men inside.

At least four to one. Not great odds.

She takes a deep breath. This is what she trained for.

And she has the element of surprise.

Her mother's voice echoes in her head. Karate. Ten years old. Trying to break through a board.

You can do it, Lee. Just focus on your hand already being through the board.

Through the board, she thinks. *You're already through the board.*

SHE SEARCHES THE ground for a weapon, finding a discarded piece of metal wire, a broken brick, and a work glove. She hangs onto it while she pans the area for its match, finding it a few yards away. Then she deals with her gown, ripping the beautiful skirt up the front and then around at thigh length.

She puts on one of the gloves and wraps the wire around it, securing one end of a garrote then slips on the other glove.

One of the guards circles around to the northwest corner of the building. He cups his hand around a cigarette, struggling to light it in the breeze. He leans in close to the shelter of the building.

She moves quickly, crossing the space between them in seconds. His back is to her. He raises his head, the finally lit cigarette dangling from his mouth, his lighter still flickering in the wind. She throws the wire over his head, bringing it up close and tight under his chin. Forcing it into his neck, she pulls hard.

The guard twists and struggles for breath, the wire cutting into his skin. His hands thrash at the wire. He heaves back and forth, but she holds on. The guard is desperate for air, so he drops to his knees, hoping to catch her off guard.

She's ready for him. She brings her knee up to his shoulder and presses down, holding him into place until he stops moving.

She takes the wire from his neck, and the guard crumples into a heap. Dead.

She finds his gun and steals his holster, slinging it over her shoulder and tucking in the weapon.

THE MAN MADE more noise than she would have liked, but hopefully not enough to be heard over the lap of water against the docks. She rounds the next corner, flat against the building to see the other guard pacing.

She waits for him to come closer then lunges, brick first, her arm swinging hard. She connects with the side of his head and hears a crack. The man goes down, stunned but not dead.

She drops her knee onto his back, wraps her gloved hand around his face, and finishes him off with a quick twist, breaking his neck then relieving him of his gun.

With the perimeter guards taken care of, there's no point in being subtle now. Once inside the building, it will be all or nothing.

She finds a door and eases it open. The warehouse is large and stinks of decaying fish. At the far end of the building is an office area with the lights on. She sees Ari and the Prince tied to chairs in the center of the room. The chairs are secured to the ground with bolts. No way for Ari to help her.

Three guards follow a woman into the office, and two more men are surrounding the captives.

Five more guards, not two.

She pushes the barrel of the gun around the door-jamb and peeks out, once again, and fires a single shot to the head, taking down one of the guards.

Then a second.

Her odds are getting better.

Her heart should be racing, but it's not. She's calm—in her element. She trained until her skills became second nature. And while the actions are the same, the stakes are different. She's not playing for a top score or bragging rights, she's playing for Ari's life and the Prince's life, as well as her own.

She hears someone yell, "Go out there and see what the hell is going on."

A guard comes out of the office, sees her, and fires

errantly—missing her by a foot. She takes aim, but he runs behind the captives for cover and is preparing to fire again. Knowing she doesn't have much time, she immediately takes off, runs up Ari's shoulder, and catapults herself into the guard, knocking him down.

While he clutches his chest trying to breathe, she fires a round into his head.

The other two guards come out of the office, and a shot rings out as one shoots his pistol toward the ceiling and says, "Stop where you are."

Except the shot doesn't have his desired effect of scaring her, rather it only causes ceiling tiles to rain down on he and his partner.

This is her chance.

She ducks down behind the captives, grips one pistol in each hand, then somersaults out, twisting and firing a gun at each of her two next targets.

Bang. Bang.

Two more down.

She crouches low, quickly scanning the area for further threats.

Ari and the Prince are in shock. They both know it's Huntley, but what she's doing—the way she flew through the air, the way she tumbled across the floor with a gun in each hand and shot two targets—is like watching a different person. A killer. A good one.

Ari is yelling against his gag, trying to tell her something. She gets the cotton out of their mouths, and he yells, "Ophelia!"

"Did they take her, too? Where is she? Where's Clarice?"

"What the hell?" asks a female voice.

Spy Girl turns. Ophelia is rushing into the room, looking around and trying to figure out what's going on.

"Ophelia, I'm here to help. Stay down while I clear the rest of the building."

"Clear the building?" She laughs as she surveys the bodies on the floor. "It appears as if you have already done that. But no matter, I can hire more where they came from."

Spy Girl swings into a tactical position. "You did this? I thought it was Clarice."

"Clarice? You think my sister could have done all this? Oh no. My sister is clueless. She's probably at home, jumping the bones of that idiot boy she thinks she's in love with."

"Where is Viktor?"

"He got a tranquilizer dart to the neck like the others. He'll wake up and assume he had one hell of a night. And then he will become King. With his father's world wide connections, there is nothing I won't have," she says, pulling a gun from her jacket and pressing it against the Prince's temple. "Drop your weapons, or I kill him now. Although, he will die soon enough. You all will."

Spy Girl has no choice. Although she's a good shot, the chance of Ophelia shooting the Prince before a bullet could kill her is too great.

She reluctantly places the guns on the floor in front of her and holds up her hands.

"You ruined your dress," Ophelia comments. "Which is fitting and slightly poetic. I can hear the account in the papers. *A torn ball gown covers the dead, would-be Princess on the night the Montrovian monarchy dies.*"

"How will you end the monarchy, Ophelia?" She knows the longer she keeps her talking the more time she has to figure out how to kill her.

"We get rid of this worthless excuse for a prince, for starters. Sorry about that. You seem to really like him. And you're nice and surprisingly good with a gun. Something that would be valuable to me in the new Montrovia."

"So your plan is to kill the Lorenzo and become Queen?"

"Absolutely. Allowing me to do whatever the hell I want. And what I want is to systematically dismantle this farce of a monarchy, starting by selling the Strait of Montrovia to the highest bidder. Once that's done, we close down our borders to these wretched tourists, shut down our port, sink all the yachts, and abolish gambling. We will ruin the country that shunned us all because—"

"All this because Daddy didn't love you?"

The Prince winces as Ophelia digs the barrel of the gun into the side of his head. "Shut up!" she says, becoming agitated. She turns her gun away from the Prince and waves it in the other direction. Exactly what Spy Girl wants.

"You don't know anything," Ophelia rants, taking a few steps toward her. "You don't know what it's like to be treated like a nobody in France when your blood is royal. If it weren't for my father's philandering ways, my mother wouldn't have taken us away to live like paupers."

While Ophelia is ranting, Spy Girl puts her hand to her chest—suddenly remembering what she tucked into her bra earlier.

"You've hardly been living like paupers here. I overheard you telling Allie that your custom dress for the Queen's Ball cost a half million euros."

"Pocket change, now. I will soon be the richest woman on the planet. The Saudis appear to be determined to own the Strait and keep upping the ante."

"You can't do that!" the Prince yells.

"Actually, I just changed my mind, the first thing I will do is tear down the Palacio de la Vallenta. Dismantle it brick by brick just like I will the monarchy." She waves the gun in his direction again, her focus back on the Prince.

That's all it takes.

Spy Girl leaps forward, first knocking Ophelia's gun to the ground and then slapping a pore strip on her forehead.

"What the hell is that?" she gasps, looking up, cross-eyed.

"Put your heads down!" Spy Girl yells to the captives as she jumps up to the ceiling, grabs the exposed metal pipe above her, and swings her body toward Ophelia. Her feet connect with Ophelia's chest, kicking her across the room as the strip explodes and blows her back into the nearby window.

When the dust settles, Spy Girl picks herself up off the ground and dusts herself off.

"What the hell was that?" the Prince yells. "How could you even—the way you shot—where did you learn all that?"

"Finishing school," she replies as Gallagher comes running into the building with his gun drawn.

He surveys the carnage, then looks at her in astonishment. "Did you do all this?"

She gives him a noncommittal shrug as sirens sound in the distance, causing her to rethink the situation. "Actually, I didn't. *You* did all of this. I was kidnapped along with the Prince and Ari. You saved us."

Gallagher studies her. Her gown is ripped and torn. Her feet are shoeless and bloody, but her hair is still perfectly coiffed and priceless jewels glitter from her neck and wrist. "I don't know what kind of look you were going for here, but it's bloody gorgeous."

She looks down at herself and smiles. "Thank you."

"How'd I do that?" He takes a peek out the broken window, where what's left of Ophelia lies.

"Explosive Band-Aid to the head. After you took out her guards, she came out of the office with a gun, threatened the Prince, and made you give up the two you had."

"Fingerprints?"

She raises her hands. "I had on these gloves the whole time. Found them in the street."

"Weapons used?"

"A wire, a brick, their guns, the Band-Aid—actually, technically it was a pore cleansing strip."

"What's that?"

"You put it on your nose to clean out your pores."

"Impressive."

"I'm really sorry I knocked you out," she says sincerely.

"It's okay. But next time we work together."

The Prince keeps looking from her to Gallagher and back again. "For God's sake, will someone untie us?"

Gallagher stares. "That all depends on you. Will you tell the same story? That I rescued the three of you?"

The Prince stares back, incredulously.

"I think Miss Von Allister would like to retain her cover, Prince Vallenta. My agency works closely with the Americans, and we had no idea she was an agent. Exactly who are you working for?" he asks, turning toward her.

"Black X," she whispers.

Ari shakes his head. "Don't lie to him, Huntley. Sir, we work for the CIA—we're undercover together. Our mission was to protect the Prince."

The Prince's eyes widen, and she can see the hurt in them. It guts her.

"I'm sorry," she says to him as the sirens get closer.

Gallagher stares at the Prince. "So, do I have your word?"

The Prince nods, silently.

Gallagher finds a rope and ties her to a chair. He waits until the police arrive to untie the Prince, who is quickly whisked back to the safety of his castle.

Ari and Huntley are briefly questioned and then driven home.

On the way there, the radio pauses for a moment of silence in honor of the passing of King Vallenta.

She knows the Prince probably hates her, but she texts him anyway, telling him she is sorry about his dad.

Then she cries.

MISSION: COMPLETE

THE DAY THAT follows is full of news reports about the Prince's kidnapping by a *rogue terror group*, his rescue by *an unnamed British agent*, the *official* story of Ophelia's death claiming she was killed during the kidnapping, and the passing of the King.

Ari and I are besieged with interview requests from reporters wanting to know about *us* being kidnapped along with the Prince.

Needless to say, we haven't responded.

OPHELIA'S MEMORIAL SERVICE is held the following day at her church in France. Her sister left Montrovia, returning home, after shockingly abdicating her right to the throne. Viktor did not attend Ophelia's funeral and hasn't been seen since. It's rumored that he was picked up by the Montrovian government, questioned, and then was allowed to privately mourn the death of his fiancée at his father's summer home on Lake Como. Intelligence believes he had no clue what Ophelia was planning.

THE COUNTRY AND the world mourn together on the third day as Montrovia lays their beloved King to rest. Ari and I are allowed to attend the funeral.

Daniel was taken to the American Embassy from the castle the night of the kidnapping, not to be heard from since.

ON THE FOURTH day, I alone receive an invitation to attend the coronation ceremony of the new King of Montrovia. The coronation is held in a massive old church on the castle grounds. While the King's funeral the day before was all black, this is a colorful affair with much pomp and circumstance. Richly hued robes worn by the bishops of the church, fully decorated military dress uniforms, banners displaying the country's flag and crest, and a choir in bright red robes. The rest of the guests are in formal attire—suits on the men, long demure gowns and hats on the women.

Although this ceremony is being televised around the world, the actual number in the church is very limited. I'm shocked I was invited.

My heart swells with pride to see Lorenzo seated on

the ornate gold throne. He stands and is draped in the Imperial Robe then sits back on the throne where he's handed the Royal Scepter and the Rod of Equity and Mercy. The crown is removed from a gilded platter and placed on his head.

"God save the King!" is shouted three times and then the bishop finishes the ceremony and pronounces Lorenzo as King of Montrovia.

Trumpets play, bells chime, gun salutes sound, and King Lorenzo Giovanni Baptiste Vallenta V of Montrovia walks proudly down the aisle with his mother and out to greet thousands of his countrymen waiting outside the church.

AFTER THE PROCESSIONAL, I find Juan standing next to me. "The King requests a word with you."

I'm escorted to the War Room and told to make myself comfortable. I give Juan back the royal jewels I wore to the Queen's Ball, then flip on the TV and watch the live footage of him greeting his fellow Montrovians. I take the fact that I'm in here and not his residence as a bad sign.

An hour later, he strolls into the room. The crown, scepter, and cape are gone, but he's still in full royal military garb. It reminds me of dancing in his arms at the Queen's Ball.

"Your Highness," I say in greeting.

"I'm sorry I haven't properly thanked you—for saving my life, saving the monarchy, and for protecting my country," he says with a sincere tone, but I can tell by his body language that he's not feeling it. He's mad at me. And I don't blame him. "But things all happened so fast—the ball, the kidnapping, my father's death, the funeral, and the coronation."

"Thanks for inviting me to your coronation. I'm honored."

"I wouldn't be here if it weren't for you. The people of Montrovia and I owe you a great debt. I had planned on bringing you here after the funeral and well, to be honest, before everything happened I was considering proposing."

"Proposing?"

"You would make a lovely princess."

"Shouldn't you marry someone you love?"

"You struck my fancy."

"We haven't even slept together."

"That was planned for somewhere between then and the proposal," he says, without a trace of a smile.

"But now?"

"I received a call from someone who wouldn't give me his name or tell me who he worked for. It was requested that I tell no one about you, not my government or even my closest confidants. They say your cover has taken years to put into place. It's my understanding you will continue to be Huntley Von Allister."

"That's correct."

"Then please get down on your knees in front of me."

I raise an eyebrow at him. "Are you looking for a royal blowjob?"

"No," he says, finally laughing at me as he takes a large sword off the wall. "I'm giving you an Accolade."

"What's that?"

"A ceremony to confer knighthood." He grins. "It's my opinion that making you Montrovian nobility will up your social status and strengthen your cover." He taps the flat side of the sword on my right shoulder, then gently raises the sword just up over my head and then taps my left shoulder. "With the power vested to me by country and crown, I make ye a knight of Montrovia."

He sets the sword aside, helps me to my feet, and kisses both my cheeks.

"I thought women couldn't be knights."

"You will be Montrovia's first, and you will be re-ferred to as the Contessa of Courtenay, a nobility title that is bestowed for your lifetime."

"So you don't hate me?"

"I owe you my life."

"That's not what I'm talking about." I touch his face and tenderly press my lips against his cheek, letting the kiss linger. "My mission was to get close to you and protect you."

"Which you did."

"Yes, but there's more you need to understand. I was taught not to become emotionally entangled—told that it only leads to failure, but I failed in that part of my mission. When I ignored you to get your attention and when I saved you, that was me the spy, but as we spent time together and I got to know you, the things I said—they were not part of the mission. Those words came from me, from my heart. I care for you, Enzo." It's the first time I've called him by his nickname. He covers my hand with his, holding it in place against his cheek. "You are going to be an amazing King."

We stand and gaze at each other.

"You and I are in the same boat," he finally says, kissing my lips in a way that feels like goodbye. "Our countries need us." He shakes his head and chuckles. "I still can't believe what you did. I've only seen people move like that in the movies."

"It was my first time," I whisper.

"Your first mission?"

"It was the first time I ever killed anyone." Tears flood my eyes. "I'm really sorry you had to see it."

He pulls me into a tight hug. "You took out seven highly-trained guards by yourself, plus Ophelia. I don't like that people had to die, either, but it was for the good of the world. The good of Montrovia. You should feel no guilt as they brought it upon themselves." He smiles and tries to change the subject. "So did you receive commendation from your country?"

"I was told to take a couple weeks vacation until my next mission."

"Hmm, somehow that doesn't seem like enough. So, I have some gifts for you, my sweet."

"I don't need presents, Lorenzo."

"Nonetheless. From my country." He hands me a passport. "You are officially a citizen of Montrovia. There are some places in the world you may travel where having an American passport is, shall we say, tricky."

"Thank you."

"From the monarchy which you saved, a monetary account has been set up in the Royal Montrovian Bank to be accessed only by your handprint. No identification is necessary. No name. A nest egg in case you decide to retire." He holds out an iPad, clicks a button, and instructs me to lay my palm on it. "Perfect."

"And from my mother, for saving her son." He hands me a deed. "The villa is now yours."

"But I thought you said you didn't tell anyone?"

"I didn't." He rolls his eyes to the ceiling, knowing he's been caught. "Fine. All the gifts are from me."

"Lorenzo, I can't accept these. I didn't do it because—" He puts his finger over my mouth to shush me.

"And that is exactly why you deserve them. I'm not

finished." He grins. "As a token of my gratitude—"

An idea flashes in my brain causing me to interrupt him. "With all the women you've dated, why haven't you dated Lady Elizabeth?"

He sighs. "I'm afraid Lizzy—how do you Americans say it—friend-zoned me when we were teens. She liked older boys."

"You're an older boy now."

He cocks his head. "You think?"

"Yeah, I do. She would make a lovely Queen."

"Yes, she would. I'll admit that I carried a bit of a torch for her in my youth."

"I could invite her over to hang out. You could show up?"

"Although that sounds lovely, I'm afraid you are due in port. Right now."

"For what?"

"Your gift from me is the use of my yacht. Do a few quiet days at sea sound good?"

"That actually sounds really nice."

"Juan will escort you there now."

"Now?"

"Yes, now."

"But I need to go home and pack."

"Your luggage is already packed and on board."

"Are you trying to get rid of me?"

"No."

"Wait, why don't you want me to go home?"

"Let's just say Ari will be—um, how do you say it—holding down the fort while you are gone."

"Did you give him a passport, too?"

"Yes. You and your brother will always have a home here." He gives me a hug. "I mean that sincerely. And if you ever need anything. Anything at all. Seriously, call me. I would do anything for you."

"Thank you, Lorenzo. That means a lot to me."

"And, now, you must go," he says, shooing me into the secret passageway from the castle down to the harbor.

WHEN I GET to the docks, I call Ellis.

"Miss Von Allister," he says, loud dance music blaring in the background.

"What's going on there? Is Ari having a party?"

"You could say a party is being had for Ari. Can't say I mind."

"Girls gone wild?"

"Very."

As I get closer to the Royal Yacht, I wonder what to expect on board. Will it be full of hot men waiting to fulfill my every desire?

I see the crew lined up for my arrival. No one else in sight.

"Good afternoon, Contessa. I'm Captain Marco. It's a pleasure to have you on board. I was told to set course for Ibiza. Unless you'd like to go somewhere else."

"No, that sounds great. And, please, call me Huntley."

As I'm shown to the owner's suite, I realize that Lorenzo knows the real me well. Knows that I crave solitude and silence. A few days at sea with the ocean breeze in my face sounds perfect, although I'm still holding out hope that he will join me at some point.

I change into a red bikini and head to the pool deck. It will be the perfect place to view the gorgeous city as we leave the harbor.

I have music playing, and I am swaying to the sounds of a sultry song as I stand next to the railing and watch my new home retreating into the distance.

A steward brings me a flute of champagne on a silver tray. I raise the glass into the air.

"You should never drink alone," a deep, sexy voice says as a strong arm snakes around my waist, pulling me back up against a muscular chest and swaying with me. "What are we drinking to?"

I turn my head and smile at him. "Montrovia."

He clinks my glass with his. "To Montrovia."

After we take a sip, I turn to face him. "Daniel, are you crashing my party?"

He flashes both of his dimples at me and says, "Baby, I *am* your party."

EPILOGUE

TERRANCE IS IN the facility underground the Montrovian villa. With the Prince safe, he can finally focus some energy on figuring out what is on the disc Huntley gave him.

With a computer he built himself that purposely has no Internet connection, he pulls up the file's content list.

He clicks on numerous files, but each one is encrypted.

He spends a few hours trying to hack his way through, but he can't unlock the code.

So he tries a different approach, pulling up the list again.

This time, he finds a single unencrypted file.

It's probably just junk.

He doesn't really expect to find anything worthwhile

when he clicks on it.

But as a picture populates the screen, he squints his eyes.

He double-checks the source of the file twice, making sure he didn't accidentally pull the photo off the computer's hard drive.

Because he's seen this before.

He looks up at the wall across from him, where Ari has photos haphazardly hung all over, and spots it.

He carries his computer over to the wall.

The photo Ari put up of the proposed Terra Project city is nearly identical to the one contained in the locket.

How in the world could Ophelia's plan to end the monarchy in Montrovia have anything to do with Huntley's mother's death in America six years ago?

ABOUT THE AUTHOR

Jillian is a *USA TODAY* bestselling author. She writes fun romances with characters her readers fall in love with, from the boy next door in the *That Boy* trilogy to the daughter of a famous actress in *The Keatyn Chronicles* series.

She's married to her college sweetheart, has two adult children, two Labs named Cali and Camber, and lives in a small Florida beach town. When she's not working, she likes to decorate, paint, doodle, shop for shoes, watch football, and go to the beach.

www.jilliandodd.net

Made in the USA
Middletown, DE
04 June 2018